Get Well Soon, Mallory!

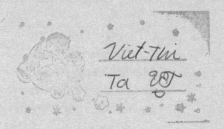

Viet-Thi
Ta

**Other books by
Ann M. Martin**

Rachel Parker, Kindergarten Show-off
Eleven Kids, One Summer
Ma and Pa Dracula
Yours Turly, Shirley
Ten Kids, No Pets
Slam Book
Just a Summer Romance
Missing Since Monday
With You and Without You
Me and Kate (the Pest)
Stage Fright
Inside Out
Bummer Summer

BABY-SITTERS LITTLE SISTER series
THE BABY-SITTERS CLUB mysteries
THE BABY-SITTERS CLUB series
(see back of the book for a more complete listing)

Get Well Soon, Mallory!
Ann M. Martin

AN
APPLE
PAPERBACK

SCHOLASTIC INC.
New York Toronto London Auckland Sydney

Cover art by Hodges Soileau

No part of this publication may be reproduced in whole or in part, or stored in a retrieval system, or transmitted in any form or by any means, electronic, mechanical, photocopying, recording, or otherwise, without written permission of the publisher. For information regarding permission, write to Scholastic Inc., 730 Broadway, New York, NY 10003.

ISBN 0-590-47007-8

12 11 10 9 8 7 6 5 4 3 2 1   3 4 5 6 7 8/9

Printed in the U.S.A.   40

First Scholastic printing, November 1993

*The author gratefully acknowledges
Jahnna Beecham and Malcolm Hillgartner
for their help in
preparing this manuscript.*

Get Well Soon, Mallory!

"Everybody, listen!" Mom shouted to my family in the living room. "I've got great news!"

Nobody heard her. They were all too busy talking at once. You see, it was Saturday, October thirtieth, the day before Halloween. Seven kids were swarming around one big trunk filled with costumes in the center of the room and let me tell you, it was a real zoo.

I'm Mallory Pike and I'm eleven, the oldest of all of those kids. Life at my house is usually pretty crazy but today things were totally bonkers. I don't know if it was all the excitement of preparing for Halloween or the cold that I had, but I was feeling pretty tired. I lay on the couch and watched as Margo, my seven-year-old sister, got into a tug-of-war with Claire, who's five and the baby of our family.

"I want to be the ballerina!" Margo cried.

"You've already been a ballerina," Claire

1

said, wrenching the tutu from Margo's hands.

Vanessa, who is nine, stepped between them. "Claire's right. It's her turn to wear the costume."

"Why don't you be a dog?" eight-year-old Nicky suggested. He was wearing a pirate's eye patch over his glasses.

"I don't want to be a dog," Margo said, pouting. "They're ugly."

"Dogs are cool," Adam shot back. Adam is one of the triplets, who are a year younger than me and identical. He gestured to Byron and Jordan, who were posed with black masks covering their eyes. "But if you don't want to be a dog, why not be a Ninja warrior with us?"

"Or a gypsy fortune teller like me?" Vanessa suggested. "I'm going to wear lots of makeup and Mom's bracelets and jewelry."

Margo liked that idea and for a moment the shouting died down. That gave Mom, who was still standing in the doorway, just enough time to make her announcement.

"Will the Pike family please try to keep it to a dull roar while I tell you my news?"

We turned to look at Mom, who smiled and said, "That's better. I just got a call from my cousins in New York."

"The Strausses?" Dad asked as he took a seat next to me on the couch.

2

Mom nodded. "Marie and Phil were both on the line. They want us to meet them in New York for Thanksgiving. We'll watch the Macy's parade, then go out for dinner."

"*The* Macy's parade?" Jordan asked, wide-eyed.

"Yes." Mom grinned. "The official parade. Phil was given bleacher seat tickets right in front of Macy's!"

"Wow! We'll get to see the groups do their dance numbers and sing their songs!" I cried.

Dad smiled. "After watching it on TV all these years, it would be fun to actually see it in person."

"A parade!" Margo picked up her toy baton and put a glitter-covered New Year's hat on her head. "That's what I'll be. A majorette. Follow me, everybody!"

Nicky and Claire fell in behind Margo and marched around the living room, singing, "We're going to the city, the city, the city, we're going to the city and we'll be on TV."

My family calls New York "the city" because it's not far from where we live in Stoneybrook, Connecticut. We only have to hop on the train and we're there in an hour or so. Of course, a family as big as mine doesn't hop on a train that often. That's why I was so excited about the idea of spending Thanksgiving in New York. I imagined us all in red-and-white-striped stocking caps and mufflers, sitting on the special bleachers oohing and ahing over the parade. I could just see Nicky making faces at the TV cameras and the triplets trying to get autographs from all of the famous people.

"Will we stay at the Strausses' apartment?" Vanessa asked, as she marched around the living room for the fourth time.

"Good heavens, no," Mom replied. "Where would they put all ten of us? No, we'll have to stay at a hotel."

"Hmmmm." Dad scratched his chin. "Things get pretty booked up around Thanksgiving. It might be tough to get reservations."

"I know." Mom pursed her lips. "And finding room for us at a restaurant could be tough, too."

I could tell by their tone of voice that they were starting to have second thoughts. Which meant that any minute they would change their minds and say we should stay home for Thanksgiving. I decided I'd better speak up.

"This is a once-in-a-lifetime chance. I'm sure some hotels are booked up by now, but New York has thousands of hotels. They can't all be full. And the same goes with restaurants."

Mom looked at Dad. "Mallory's got a point."

"It might take a few more calls," I said. "But

4

I bet we could get reservations. Do you want me to help call?"

Mom sat on the couch next to me and felt my forehead. "No, I think you should rest. You look a little tired."

I hated to admit it but I didn't feel just a little tired, I felt a lot tired. It must have been this virus I caught after Dawn (one of our BSC members), moved back to California. What's the BSC? It stands for the Baby-sitters Club, which is just about the most important thing in my life. But I'll tell you about our club later.

Anyway, I'd been feeling really rundown lately. I know I must sound like one of those Geritol commercials for old people but I'm serious. Sometimes I could barely keep my eyes open in class. When I came home from school, I was too tired to do my homework or even watch TV or eat dinner. And if anyone in my family gets the teeniest, tiniest little cold, I catch it. I just wished I would get over this.

I spent the rest of Saturday night on the couch watching the Halloween modeling show. First Margo was a majorette, then a cowgirl, then a mermaid, and finally a princess. I think I fell asleep while she was looking for construction paper to make her crown.

Dad must have carried me to my room because I woke up the next morning in my bed.

"Happy Halloween!" Nicky shouted through a paper towel holder he had aimed at my ear.

I fumbled to find my glasses. (Yes, I'm four-eyed. I want to get contacts but my parents won't let me.) Then I looked at the clock. It was nearly eleven. I'd missed breakfast and my morning chores!

"Where is everybody?" I mumbled to Nicky as I shuffled to my closet for my robe.

"Dad and the triplets are in the garage making wooden swords. They decided to be pirates."

"I thought you were going to be a pirate," I muttered.

"That was yesterday." Nicky leaped in front of me at the top of the stairs and struck a pose with his arms folded across his chest. "Now I'm Aladdin."

We passed my parents' room where Vanessa was sitting on Mom's dresser in front of the mirror, waving. But she wasn't waving to us. She was waving at the mirror.

"Vanessa, who are you waving at?" I asked.

My voice startled her so much that she nearly fell off the dresser. When she saw me, her cheeks turned a bright pink and she murmured, "The cameras."

6

"What cameras?" I asked.

"The ones at the parade on Thanksgiving," she said, hopping off the dresser. "I called my friend Liza last night and told her we were going to be at the parade and she said to start practicing my wave."

"Why do you need to practice?" I asked. "A wave's a wave."

"No, Liza said there are three types of waves," Vanessa explained. "The windshield wiper, screwing in the light bulb, and the flap." Vanessa demonstrated them as she spoke. The windshield wiper looked like its name, and so did the flap, which consisted of her flapping her hand up and down. But the lightbulb seemed a bit more complicated.

"The Queen of England uses the light bulb one," Vanessa said, eyeing her reflection once more. "It's the hardest to do because you have to hold your hand in a wave position as you turn your wrist back and forth, like you were screwing in a lightbulb."

Nicky and I joined Vanessa at the mirror, practicing our waves, until Mom came in and found us. When we explained that we were practicing our waves for the cameras, Mom clasped her hands in front of her and put on her really serious look, the one she wears when she delivers bad news.

"What makes you so sure we're going to the parade?" Mom asked.

"Oh, no," Vanessa gasped. "We have to go. I've told all of my friends. It'd be too embarrassing if we stayed home."

A smile crept around the corners of Mom's mouth. "We've found a hotel that can take us. We're just waiting to hear from a restaurant your father called. If they can fit us in then we'll go."

"I'll keep my fingers crossed," I said.

The rest of the day was spent getting ready for Halloween. Claire had slept in her pink tutu the night before and skipped around the house all afternoon, chanting, "Trick or treat, trick or treat, give us something good to eat!"

At four o'clock, the triplets appeared at the top of the stairs in full pirate dress. Each wore a bandanna on his head and a black patch over one eye. Jordan had even found an old fake parrot in a trunk in our attic and pinned it to his shoulder.

"*Arrrgh!*" they all shouted at once.

Nicky was right behind them. He wore a towel turban that kept slipping down over one eye and had slipped Mom's copper bracelet on his left arm. Claire's tutu was wrinkled but she didn't care. Margo's paper princess crown looked wonderful (even though it did shower glitter every time she moved), and Vanessa's gypsy outfit was her best ever. Big gold clip-on earrings dangled from her ears and she'd teased her hair so it stuck out at the sides.

"You kids look great," Dad said as he arranged them on the stairs for a group photograph. "After this shot I'll tell you my good news."

Dad didn't get a chance to announce it because Nicky yelled it first. "We're going to New York for Thanksgiving!"

"That's right, and we'll be staying at the —"

The cheering drowned out the rest of his sentence. Margo and Nicky hugged each other. The triplets gave everyone high and low fives. Vanessa hugged me, then made a beeline for the phone. She had to call her friend Liza and gloat.

The kids chattered nonstop about the New York trip as Dad and I got them ready to leave the house. My best friend Jessica Ramsey and I had planned to take her little brother and sister out, but by the time I'd passed around bags and talked Claire into wearing a coat over her tutu, I was too exhausted to walk anywhere. So I gave Jessi a call.

"I think I'm going to stay home tonight. I'm really tired," I said.

"What'd you do?" she asked. "Stay up late last night?"

"No, I fell asleep after dinner and didn't

9

wake up till eleven this morning."

"That's strange," Jessi said. "Are you sick?"

I felt my forehead. It didn't feel unusually warm. "I don't have a fever, or anything like that," I explained. "I just feel worn out."

"Well, you better not come with us, then. Squirt and Becca are so excited, they'll probably run the entire night."

(Squirt is the nickname for Jessi's baby brother, who's only about a year and a half. Becca's her eight-and-a-half-year-old sister who looks like a younger version of Jessi.)

"Sorry to back out on you," I mumbled.

"That's okay," Jessi replied. "I understand."

"Oh, guess what. One more thing," I said before we hung up. "My family's going to New York for Thanksgiving and we get to watch the parade from special bleacher seats right in front of Macy's. We might be on TV."

"Mal, that's fantastic!" Jessi squealed.

I wished I was as enthusiastic about it as Jessi sounded, but I just didn't feel it. I had a really uneasy feeling inside. Something awful had just occured to me. What if I was still sick in three weeks? I couldn't travel all that way and feel this lousy. I'd ruin the whole vacation.

Jessi and I said good-bye and I sat at my desk, trying to catch up on my work. I'd missed a lot of school as I caught cold after cold and the homework had really started to pile up. The more I stared at my math, the more blurry-eyed I felt. Finally I shut my math book and lay my head on top of the desk. I decided to take a little nap before the trick-or-treaters started ringing our bell.

I slept through Halloween! Can you believe it? The members of the Baby-sitters Club couldn't, when I told them at Claudia Kishi's house on Monday afternoon.

"How could that happen?" Stacey McGill asked. "Your doorbell must have been ringing nonstop for hours. Ours sure was."

All I could do was shrug. "I guess I was pretty tired."

"Tired!" Claudia repeated. "You must have been catatonic!"

Before anybody could make another remark, the digital clock on Claudia's dresser turned from 5:29 to 5:30 and Kristy Thomas, who was wearing her visor and sitting in the director's chair, announced, "All right, everybody. This meeting of the BSC has officially started."

I think now would be a perfect time to tell you about our club. It was Kristy's great idea (she has a zillion of them). The club began after Kristy heard her mom making phone call after phone call to find a sitter for her younger brother, David Michael. Kristy thought, why not form a club so that a client could make one call and reach several sitters? She told her idea to her best friend, Mary Anne Spier, and also to Claudia, who told Stacey McGill, and — *ta, da!* — the Baby-sitters Club was born.

Kristy was elected president, partly because the club was her idea but also because she's a born leader. She's loaded with energy and she has a big mouth. (I'm not being mean. She'd be the first to admit it.) Kristy has brown hair, brown eyes, and is very short. I think she's the shortest girl in the eighth grade. She's a real tomboy and generally dresses in her standard uniform of jeans, turtleneck, pullover sweater, and sneakers. Kristy loves sports. In fact, she coaches a softball team called Kristy's Krushers. The Krushers play the Bashers quite a bit, which brings me to Bart Taylor. The Bashers are his team. He's Kristy's sort-of boyfriend. (I say sort-of because she would never *call* him her boyfriend. But they do go to dances and stuff together.)

Kristy has almost as many people in her family as I do in mine. But it wasn't always that way. First there was just her mom and her three brothers: Charlie (sixteen), Sam (fourteen), and seven-year-old David Michael.

Kristy's father walked out on their family right after David Michael was born and she never hears from him. It was kind of a struggle for Kristy's mom to support four kids but a year or so ago she met Watson Brewer. Are you ready for this? He's a real millionaire. Mrs. Thomas fell in love with Watson, who already had two kids of his own — Andrew and Karen — and they got married. Then they adopted Emily Michelle, a two-year-old Vietnamese girl, which is why Kristy's grandmother Nannie came to live with them. So on some weekends, when Andrew and Karen are visiting, ten people are at Kristy's house. They're lucky they live in a mansion!

You know the saying, opposites attract? Well, it must be true because Kristy's best friend is Mary Anne Spier (our club secretary) who is one of the shyest people on the planet. Mary Anne is also very emotional. She'll cry at anything — a sad movie, or a picture of cute kittens. Mary Anne likes all animals but has a soft spot for cats, particularly her black-and-white striped kitten named Tigger.

Mary Anne's mom died when she was little so she was raised by her dad, who used to be really strict. He wouldn't let her talk on the phone or stay out late and for awhile her clothes were really babyish. But that's all changed. He married his high school sweet-

14

heart, who just happens to be the divorced mother of Mary Anne's other best friend, Dawn Schafer. (Dawn was the BSC's alternate officer — she filled in for anyone who had to miss a meeting — until she left but I'll tell you about that in a minute.) Let's see, after the wedding, Mary Anne (who had become Dawn's stepsister) and Mr. Spier moved in with Dawn and her mom, who lived in this old farmhouse that has a real secret passage. (It might even be haunted.)

They were all pretty happy until a short while ago when Dawn really started missing her dad and her brother Jeff, who live in California. Dawn asked her mom if she could stay with them for several months. It was a tough decision for everyone involved, but finally it was agreed that she could go. Even though Dawn had been happy here, she'd always been a California girl at heart. We all miss her a lot but I'm sure Mary Anne misses her the most.

When Dawn left for California our club went through a rough time trying to figure out how to replace her. Shannon Kilbourne was an associate member which meant that she just took sitting jobs when the regular club members were extra busy or if we suddenly got a lot of job calls. Shannon is really interesting looking. She has curly blonde hair, blue eyes (that look startling because she wears black mascara), a ski jump nose and super high cheekbones. She lives near Kristy and goes to Stoneybrook Day School, a private school across town. (The rest of us go to Stoneybrook Middle School.) When Kristy first moved to Watson's mansion she thought Shannon and the other girls in the neighborhood were real snobs but it turned out to be just a big misunderstanding. Now Shannon and Kristy are friends and the best news is that Shannon is able to come to meetings and fill in for Dawn while she's in California. And we still have one associate member left. His name is Logan Bruno, and guess what. He's Mary Anne's boyfriend.

That brings me to Claudia. Claud is vice-president of the BSC mostly because she not only has her own phone but also her own number. Isn't that cool? That's why we hold the meetings at her house. Our clients can reach us easily. Claudia is Japanese-American and really gorgeous. She has this straight shiny black hair and big almond-shaped eyes and, because Claud is an artist, everything she wears looks really stylish. She makes her own earrings, which can be little dangly papier-mâché stars and a moon with a cow jumping over it, or paper clips and safety pins painted in neon colors. Claud has a perfect ivory complexion, which is amazing because she is com-

16

pletely addicted to junk food. I'm not kidding! Ring Dings, Malomars, Twinkies — she's hidden them all over her room.

Claud is very creative and smart, but she's not the best student in the world. English is her worst subject (she used to be a terrible speller but she's getting better). Part of the reason Claudia has trouble in school may have something to do with the fact that her sister Janine is a genius and Claud doesn't want to compete with her. Janine is a junior in high school but (are you ready for this?) she's already taking courses at college!

Stacey McGill is Claudia's best friend and the BSC treasurer because she's really good in math. Stacey grew up in New York City and is the most sophisticated member of our group. She wears super trendy clothes and her long blonde hair is permed. She has big blue eyes and is tall and thin.

Stacey sounds perfect, doesn't she? But she has a problem which is really serious. Stacey is diabetic, which means her body can't process sugar. So she has to stay away from sweets and watch her diet. If she doesn't get enough of something called insulin every day her body could get all out of whack and Stacey could get really sick. Here's the yucky part — she has to give herself injections every single day. (Ew! ew!) I don't know how she does it.

17

Stacey's home life has been pretty bumpy lately. First her parents moved to Stoneybrook, then they moved back to New York City. Then they got a divorce (which was traumatic for Stacey) and then Stacey had to decide whether to live with her mom or her dad. We're all glad she chose her mom because her mom moved back to Stoneybrook. Guess what? We're neighbors. The McGills moved into the house directly behind mine. Stacey and I have a special code that we use on school days. If I leave a white towel on my patio, it means, "Let's walk to school together." A red towel means that I have to walk my brothers and sisters to school.

There are two other members of the BSC — me and Jessica Ramsey. Because we're only eleven and in the sixth grade (the other members are thirteen-year-old eighth-graders) and can only baby-sit on weekends or afternoons, we're called junior officers.

Jessi and I are a lot alike. We love to read, especially horse stories by Marguerite Henry. We're each the oldest kid in our family and we both finally convinced our parents to let us get our ears pierced. Jessi and I are also very different. I love writing and plan to be a famous children's book author and illustrator someday. Jessi loves ballet and intends to become a famous ballerina. She will, too.

Jessi goes to a special dance school in nearby Stamford, Connecticut, and already has danced many important lead parts. (You should see her dance; she's amazing.) Oh, one other difference: our looks. Jessi is black, with beautiful long legs and big brown eyes. I'm white, with short legs, glasses, and frizzy red hair.

And that's our club.

"Any new business?" Kristy asked from her director's chair.

Ever since Mom had made the announcement that we were going to see the Macy's parade, all I could think about was Thanksgiving. I brought it up.

"I'm going to be gone for the entire Thanksgiving weekend, Mary Anne, so be sure not to schedule me for any jobs."

"Where are you going?" Mary Anne asked as she jotted down my news in the club notebook. As secretary, Mary Anne keeps track of all of our schedules so when a client calls she knows which of us are available. It's hard to believe but Mary Anne has *never* made a scheduling mistake.

"New York City," I said. "One of our relatives got us bleacher seats to watch the Macy's parade."

"How fun!" Claudia said. "I wish I could go."

"My parents and I used to go to the parade every year," Stacey said wistfully. "You're going to love it."

"Speaking of Thanksgiving," Kristy said, chewing thoughtfully on her pencil, "I've got this idea — "

"Uh, oh," Claudia cut in. "You know what happens when Kristy gets one of her great ideas."

"Yeah." Stacey laughed. "We all have to do it. And it nearly kills us."

"Cut it out, you guys." Kristy waved a hand at Stacey. "I was just thinking about the meaning of Thanksgiving. Every year we all have wonderful Thanksgiving dinners with our families. But there are people out there who don't have families. Wouldn't it be great if this year we did something special for them?"

"You mean like people in homeless shelters?" Shannon asked.

Kristy nodded.

"Or the people at Stoneybrook Manor," Claudia said. "I know some of them don't have any families or friends." (Stoneybrook Manor is a residence for elderly people.)

"That's it!" Kristy said. "We could do something for the Manor. We already know a lot of the people there like Esther Barnard, Karen's friend from her school's adopt-a-grandparent program."

20

"That's right," Stacey said. "We could talk to Mrs. Fellows, the activities director, or to Ruth. Remember, she took care of Mr. Hennessey when he lived there?

Mr. Hennessey was this frail old man who told Stacey and the rest of us mysterious tales about the haunted house he had once lived in on Elm Street.

"My uncle Joe would be able to tell us what the residents like," I said. "I'll ask him the next time we visit him." Uncle Joe is my dad's uncle. He lived in a couple of homes before he moved to Stoneybrook. He even stayed with my family for a few weeks and boy, was that tough. He seemed really cranky but we found out later that he was developing Alzheimer's disease. Uncle Joe wasn't used to being around kids (and we've got a lot of them).

"Hey, what if we got our sitting charges involved in our Thanksgiving plans?" Mary Anne said. "It would be fun for the old people at the Manor and a good way for the kids to learn about Thanksgiving."

Kristy grinned at Mary Anne. "Brilliant. I wish I'd thought of it."

"Kristy, you always have the great ideas," Claudia kidded. "It's nice to spread them around."

We didn't get to talk much more about our

21

Thanksgiving plans because the phone started ringing and didn't stop until it was six o'clock on the dot. A lot of baby-sitting assignments were made. Phew! I felt tired just thinking about them.

I rode my bike home that afternoon feeling more dragged out than ever. It took forever to get home and once there, I barely had enough strength to climb the steps to my front door. All I could think about was the nap I was going to take when I got inside. What was wrong with me?

CHAPTER 3

It was Tuesday morning, and I hurt all over. Everything hurt. I mean, *every*thing. My joints, my skin — even my hair hurt. I stumbled over to look in the mirror above my dresser. I opened my mouth and said, "Ah." My throat was fiery red and burned every time I tried to swallow. Two bumps stuck out of my neck, just under my ears. My glands had swollen to the size of big marbles.

I desperately wanted to crawl back in bed but I couldn't. It was a school day and I had two tests that I just couldn't miss. Besides, I'd already missed so much school that I was starting to think I'd never catch up. I glanced at Vanessa's bed and saw that she was already up. She was probably eating breakfast. I hoped I wasn't going to be late.

"The Barretts," I muttered as I shuffled to my closet. I was scheduled to sit for them after school. I was going to have to muster every

23

ounce of strength to take care of those three. They're a real handful.

I grabbed the first thing my hand touched inside the closet, a sweatshirt. I tugged it over my head and sat down on the bed. I felt a little dizzy. Then the simple effort of pulling on a pair of jeans and slipping on my socks made little beads of sweat pop out along my forehead. I'd been sick before but this was the worst I'd ever felt. It was going to be a long day.

It seemed to take hours to finish getting dressed and go downstairs to the breakfast table. As I pulled out a chair, Claire looked up at me and announced, "Ew, Mallory's all sweaty — and look at her face. She looks like a ghost."

Mom took one look at me and ordered, "Back to bed."

"But my tests . . . the Barretts . . ." I mumbled as she guided me toward the stairs.

"I'll take care of all that," Mom replied. "Now, I want you to lie down while I find the thermometer."

Mom took my temperature. It was 103°. No wonder I was sweating. I lay back and dozed while Mom called the school and then made arrangements for Stacey to take my sitting job at the Barretts'. The next thing I knew, I was lying on the couch in Dr. Dellenkamp's waiting room.

"Well, Mallory," Dr. Dellenkamp said as she peered at my tonsils, "you have the distinction of having one of the worst looking throats I've ever seen."

"Nnnngh," was all I could say because the tongue depressor was still in my mouth.

"You probably have strep throat, a bacterial infection, or mononucleosis."

Any one of the three sounded terrible. Dr. Dellenkamp did a quick in-office strep test which came out negative. That left two options. She stuck a pin in my finger (I was too sick to feel it) and drew a blood sample.

"The blood test will tell us what you have, but in case our strep test was inaccurate or you have a bacterial infection, I'm going to start you on antibiotics right away."

"Great," I mumbled. Anything that would make my throat and body stop hurting sounded good to me.

"We should get the blood test result back in a couple of days. In the meantime, I want you to be sure and stay in bed, drink plenty of fluids, and take some Tylenol for your fever or headache."

After a quick stop at the pharmacy and then the grocery store to stock up on orange and apple juice, Mom took me home and I crawled back under the covers. The rest of Tuesday evaporated in a dreamy blur.

On Wednesday I discovered that while I was sleeping, Mom and Dad had moved Vanessa in with Claire and Margo.

"Mallory needs to be by herself so she can get plenty of rest," Mom explained to the rest of my brothers and sisters. "And if what she's got is contagious, we want to try to keep the rest of you from getting it."

By Wednesday afternoon I felt a little better. The Tylenol seemed to help my headache and it didn't hurt quite so much to swallow. But it was weird. Before, when I had taken antibiotics for an ear infection or a strep throat, they made a big difference. This time they didn't. I still felt achy and exhausted.

When the clock beside my bed turned from 5:29 to 5:30 I got this really strange feeling. Everyone in the BSC was gathered at Claud's. It didn't seem right that I was still at home. I decided I'd better call and report in.

"Baby-sitters Club," Stacey answered in her official-sounding voice.

"Hi, Stacey," I croaked. "It's Mallory."

"Hey, everybody," she called to the room. "It's Mal!"

I heard shouts of, "Hi, Mal! How are you feeling? Are you getting better?" in the background and I couldn't help smiling.

"I don't know what's the matter with me, but I still feel pretty rotten," I answered. "I don't think I'll be able to go to any of my jobs this week."

Kristy grabbed the phone. "Don't worry, Mal. We've worked it all out. Logan's here with us and we'll cover for you."

"Thanks," I murmured. "I really appreciate it."

The next person on the line was Jessi. "Mallory, everybody asks about you at school. How are you doing?"

"Not great," I said. "And I'm really worried about homework. Mom's been getting it for me, but I'm just too tired to do it."

"Then don't," Jessi said. "The important thing is for you to rest and get better. Don't worry about it."

"I'll try not to," I said. But when I hung up the phone and looked at the big stack of books and assignments from school piled up on my desk, I felt like crying. How would I ever catch up?

On Friday we got the official news.

"Mallory can stop taking the antibiotics," Dr. Dellenkamp told my mom. "She has mononucleosis."

"What can we do?" Mom asked.

"Unfortunately, nothing except keep her in

27

bed. Mallory needs to stay there until her throat and glands are completely back to normal."

Mom talked to Dr. Dellenkamp for ten more minutes before she hung up. When she told me what I had, I said, "I've never heard of mononucleosis. What is it?"

"Mono is sometimes called glandular fever," she explained, "which means it affects the lymph nodes."

"Is that why my neck looks like I've got golf balls sticking out of it?"

"Yes. The good news is, ninety-nine percent of the time it's not serious if you take care of yourself, which means staying in bed."

"And if I don't?"

"Well, sometimes too much activity can cause damage to your spleen."

That sounded scary even though at that moment I had no idea what my spleen was. Or where it was. I looked it up later in our encyclopedia and found out that the spleen is a soft, purplish-red organ (ew, ick!) located in the upper part of the abdominal cavity. It's close to the stomach and to the diaphragm. They don't really know what it does but they do know that it acts like a lymph gland and has a lot to do with our immune system.

"How long do I have to stay in bed?" I asked, figuring I'd be there through the weekend and go back to school on Monday.

Mom pursed her lips. "As little as a week. Or it could be a month or so. We don't know."

"A month!" I gasped, dropping my head back on my pillow. "I'm going to flunk out of school! I'll be in sixth grade for the rest of my life!"

Mom smoothed her hand over my forehead. "Now don't get upset, it will only make you feel worse. You're not going to fail. I'll make sure of that."

I tried to believe her but I was too worried. And what I heard next only made me more upset.

"Mallory has the kissing disease!" Jordan shouted as the triplets arrived home from school.

"The kissing disease?" I looked at Mom. "Is that what I have? But I haven't kissed anyone."

"It's only called the kissing disease because it's mostly teenagers who get it."

"But what will the kids at school think?"

I was answered by Nicky who banged through my bedroom door and chanted, "Mallory has cooties! Mallory has cooties!"

"Nicky," Mom said shooing him out of the room. "That's enough. Mallory does not have cooties."

"Then why can't Vanessa sleep in her room?" he asked.

"Because there's a slight chance that you kids could catch mono if Mallory is still in the infectious state."

"See?" Nicky said. "She does have cooties."

"Stay away from me," Adam shouted, holding up his arms in the shape of a cross as if I were a vampire.

Then Vanessa stuck her head in my room. "Mallory, you should hear what the kids are saying to Ben Hobart. They say he kissed you and gave you the disease."

"*What?* I never kissed Ben." I turned to Mom. "Make them stop. I swear I never kissed anybody."

"Cooties, cooties, Mallory has the cooties," Claire chanted. It was almost too much to bear.

I pulled my pillow over my head. Now I had much bigger things to worry about than homework. How would I ever be able to face the kids at school when every student and teacher at Stoneybrook Middle School knew that I, Mallory Pike, had the kissing disease?

CHAPTER 4

Saturday

Boy, has Charlotte Johanssen come a long way! It's hard to believe she was ever a shy little girl clinging to her mom's leg. We spent almost all of Saturday together and I felt more like her older sister than her sitter. We talked nonstop and had a great time. It was a perfect fall day — cool, but sunny. We put on our jackets and took a stroll into town. And that's where Char came up with her brilliant idea.

Stacey and Charlotte Johanssen have always had a special relationship. It might have something to do with the fact that they're both only children or that Char's mom is a doctor and helped Stacey and her family when Stacey was coming to terms with her diabetes. Char used to be extremely quiet and sad and didn't have any friends. But with Stacey's help she's now happy, much more outgoing, and has lots of friends.

Anyway, it was Saturday, and Charlotte was wearing a cranberry-colored felt beret (just like Stacey's) over her long chestnut brown hair. She slipped her gloved hand into Stacey's as they walked down the street toward town.

"Stacey, do you think the Pilgrims dressed in those black clothes with the big white collars and pointy hats because they thought they looked good, or because they had to?"

"I don't know, Char." Stacey chuckled. "What made you ask that?"

"Well, we're putting on a Thanksgiving play at school, and Bobby Phillips said Pilgrim kids wouldn't have worn those dorky outfits."

"What does Bobby think they wore?"

"He said the Pilgrim kids would probably have dressed more like the Indians, because that way they could climb trees and build forts much easier."

"It makes sense," Stacey said. "But the Pilgrims were very strict and I'm sure they thought what they wore was not dorky."

"I would have hated it," Charlotte declared. "Dresses to the floor and those silly hats and no colors. Ick."

Stacey gave Charlotte's hand a squeeze. "I'm with you."

"Our play is the Wednesday before Thanksgiving," Char continued. "Can you come?"

"I'll have to check my schedule with the BSC," Stacey replied. "But I'll sure try. Who do you play?"

Charlotte blinked her big brown eyes at Stacey and said very seriously, "The head turkey."

"What does the head turkey do?"

"Well, a head turkey in real life would probably lead all the turkeys away from the hunters and help them find good places to hide, but in our play the head turkey leads the turkey dance."

The thought of Charlotte Johanssen in a turkey costume leading a bunch of other turkeys in a dance sounded pretty funny. "The turkeys are going to dance?" Stacey said. "I wouldn't miss this for the world. On Monday I'm going to tell Mary Anne not to schedule me for anything the day before Thanksgiving."

"Thanks, Stacey," Charlotte said. "I'll try not to mess up any steps."

"I'm sure you'll be wonderful."

The two of them had reached downtown Stoneybrook, which is about fifteen minutes from the Johanssens' house. Because Thanksgiving was only a few weeks away the main street had taken on a festive look. It seemed as though every shop window was decorated for the holiday.

"Where should we go first?" Stacey asked. Charlotte saw the twinkle in Stacey's eye and the two of them answered the question at the same time.

"Polly's!"

The official name of the store is Polly's Fine Candy and it is famous all over Connecticut not only for its delicious sweets but for its wonderful window displays.

Stacey and Charlotte made their way down the street and stopped one store away from the shop with its red-and-white-striped awning.

"Close your eyes," Stacey instructed. Charlotte squeezed her lids closed. "Now what do you smell?"

Charlotte took a deep breath. "Chocolate.

Mmmm! And saltwater taffy . . . and roasted hazel nuts."

"It smells divine," Stacey said.

Charlotte opened her eyes and repeated after Stacey, "Divine!"

Stacey can't eat sweets but that doesn't mean she doesn't like them. She loves them. Especially chocolate. It takes a lot of willpower for her to not eat it.

"Come on, Stacey!" Charlotte pulled Stacey down the street. "Let's look in the window."

The year before, Polly's Thanksgiving window display had featured a huge chocolate turkey surrounded by lots of little chocolate turkeys and it was spectacular. But this year, Polly had really outdone herself.

"Oh, Stacey, look!" Charlotte exclaimed. "It's the Mayflower filled with Pilgrims, and the Indians waiting for them at Plymouth Rock. All in chocolate!"

"Wow." Stacey pointed to a plaque in the corner of the window. "Look. They won first prize in The Chocolatiers of America sculpting contest."

"I can see why," Charlotte murmured. Her eyes were two huge saucers as she oohed and ahed over every detail.

"The ship has a chocolate steering wheel and a chocolate flag — "

"And a mouse!" Stacey cried. "Look, Char! Behind those chocolate barrels and crates, they put a tiny little chocolate mouse."

The two of them spent fifteen minutes looking in Polly's windows. To the right of the front door was a much smaller window holding a lovely gingerbread house with elaborate grillwork made of icing. A gumdrop Santa was perched on the roof as a reminder that Christmas would be coming soon after Thanksgiving.

"Boy, that was fun," Charlotte said as they finally pulled themselves away from the window display and moved on to the next shop. "I can't wait for Thanksgiving to get here."

"Me neither," Stacey agreed. "Especially this year. You see, my friends and I decided to try to do something for others this year."

"What others?" Charlotte asked.

"Well, there are lots of people in need, but we thought we'd try to do something very special for the old people at Stoneybrook Manor. Not only that, we want to get you and some of the other kids involved."

Charlotte cocked her head and thought about it. "I'd like that."

"We haven't settled on a project yet," Stacey continued. "We're all supposed to come up with suggestions."

"Well, a visit from us kids would definitely

be nice," Charlotte said. "It must get awfully lonely for those people whose grandchildren live in other states."

"But what should we do when we visit?"

"How about bringing them presents?" Charlotte said, eyeing a shop window with a Christmas display of a sleigh full of presents covered in red and green foil. "Everyone likes gifts."

"But they'll be getting presents for Christmas."

"How about Thanksgiving-type presents? You know, a cone basket full of food."

"You mean, a cornucopia?" Stacey giggled.

"That's it. That basket shaped like a horn."

"Hmm." Stacey squinted one eye shut. "It would be hard to find that many cornucopias. But baskets would work."

"We could fill them with special treats to eat," Charlotte added.

"Char!" Stacey gave her a hug. "I think you've just solved our problem!"

Stacey and Charlotte continued to walk down Main Street but neither of them noticed any of the other window displays. They were too busy discussing the details of how to make goody baskets for Stoneybrook Manor.

"This is a big project," Stacey said. "I wonder if we'd be able to make enough baskets for all the residents?"

"I'll help," Charlotte said. "And I bet Becca Ramsey, and Nicky and Margo Pike will, too."

"If all the BSC members worked on it, plus the kids," Stacey murmured, "we just might be able to pull it off. Now let's see. What should we put in each basket?"

"Chocolate," Charlotte declared. "Everybody likes chocolate."

Stacey ruffled Charlotte's hair. "But not everyone can eat it. Some elderly people are on diets as strict as mine."

"Then put fruit and cheeses and healthy things in, too."

By this time the girls were back at the Johanssens'. Stacey fixed a snack of ants on a log (celery, cream cheese, and raisins). Then she and Charlotte got out pencils and paper and sat down at the coffee table in front of the couch to make a list.

"The big question is," Stacey said, nibbling thoughtfully on her eraser, "how do we pay for all this stuff?"

"Maybe people will give the food to us free," Charlotte said. "There are lots of things in our house that we don't eat."

"Food drive," Stacey said as she wrote it on her paper. "That will help. But there are some things, like fruit, that people don't just have sitting around their houses. We may need to do some sort of fundraiser."

"A fundraiser *and* make up the baskets?" Charlotte repeated. "That's a lot of work."

"I know, I know." Stacey leaned back against the couch. "It's a little scary, isn't it?"

Charlotte nodded and then grinned, revealing her dimples. "But really exciting!"

Stacey could hardly wait to get home to share Charlotte's idea with the rest of the BSC. Of course, she dialed Kristy first.

"Charlotte Johanssen just came up with the best idea for Stoneybrook Manor. What do you think of making goody baskets that we fill with food, and maybe even a surprise or two?"

Kristy didn't hesitate for a second. "Great idea," she said.

"The only problem," Stacey continued, "is how to pay for the baskets. We could have a fundraiser, or we could ask for donations."

"I think we should do both," Kristy said. "We'll come up with the specifics later. Right now I'll call Shannon and Mary Anne. Then Mary Anne can call Logan — "

"And I'll call Claudia," Stacey said. "And Jessi and Mallory."

"Spread the news about the goody baskets," Kristy instructed. "Tell everyone to start thinking about a fundraiser and we'll talk on Monday."

That night the phone lines were busy all over town. I was the last person Stacey called.

Mom and Dad had plugged our downstairs phone into the jack in my room so I wouldn't have to get out of bed.

"I think it's a terrific idea," I said to Stacey. "But I don't think I'm going to be able to make Monday's meeting."

"You don't have to," Stacey said. "I just want you to think about ways we can raise money to pay for the baskets."

"There aren't many things the doctor will let me do," I joked. "But thinking is one of them. I've got plenty of time for that."

"Good. And if you come up with a brilliant fundraising scheme, call me."

I didn't think I was capable of coming up with anything brilliant ever again, but I said I would call, anyway.

After Stacey had finished her calls she checked in with Kristy. "Everybody I talked to is excited about the project," Kristy said. "I can't wait to get started!"

Before Stacey went to bed that night she made one last call.

"Dr. Johanssen?" she said. "This is Stacey. I know Char's in bed by now, but when she wakes up tomorrow, please tell her that everyone in the BSC absolutely loved her idea!"

CHAPTER 5

I used to like my pajamas. They're made of white flannel, with tiny pink rosebuds printed all over them, and pink lace at the collar and cuffs. Mom said they were "practical but feminine" and I agreed. Well, after a week of lying around in bed staring at the tiny little rosebuds and the lacy cuffs, I wanted to tear them up and burn them.

After I burned my pajamas, I planned to blow up the television set. At first, having the portable TV in my room was kind of neat, but how many soap operas can a person watch? What gets me is nothing ever happens until Friday. Then on Friday one of the characters announces that he's getting a divorce or quitting his job, or that she's going to have a baby. I know they do that just so you'll tune in on Monday (which I did, because there wasn't anything else to do).

My brothers and sisters had been great. For

a solid week they'd tiptoed past my room and spoken in hushed tones, as if I were a patient in a hospital. In fact, Margo and Claire had even decorated my room to look like a hospital room. They'd attached a clipboard to the end of my bed, and brought up one of the house-plants from downstairs and placed it on a table beside the bed. Whenever any of the other kids wanted to talk to me, Margo would tap lightly on the door, stick her head in the room, and announce, "Mallory, you have a visitor."

I did get to go downstairs a couple of times (whoopee) and once I even went to the base-ment to see a show that Margo, Nicky, and Claire had put together just for me. It was called "Mallory Is Sick." Claire played me and her part consisted of lying on a cot pretending to be asleep. Margo and Nicky played the doc-tors who discovered I had cooties. They talked a lot about operating while they mixed up a drink of milk, orange juice, and raisins. It was supposed to be a miracle cure for the cooties. Then they tried to make Claire drink it but she refused, so the show ended in an argument. I know it was supposed to make me feel better but I was too tired to laugh.

"Mom," I complained as I shuffled back to my bedroom, "why do the kids keep saying I have cooties?"

"Because they can't pronounce mononucleosis," she said with a smile.

"Why don't they just call it mono like everyone else?"

Mom shrugged. "Cooties is more fun."

"Fun for who?" I grumbled as I got back into bed. "Not me. I can't remember what fun feels like."

Mom tucked the covers up around my neck. "Just get some rest and later on you can try to do a little homework."

"Homework."

Just saying the word made me tired. I had been trying to keep up with my schoolwork but it was hard to concentrate. I'd work on a few math problems and discover that my pencil had drifted off the page and I'd drooled on the paper (ew, gross).

On Saturday Mom tapped on my door. "Mal? Your father and I are taking the older kids into town to do some shopping. Do you mind keeping an eye on Margo and Claire?"

"Mind!" I sat up in bed. "I'd love to." At last, something to do besides lie on my back, watch TV, and try to do homework!

"Make sure they get something to eat," my mother said. "I put some cheese sandwiches in the fridge for lunch. And if they want a snack, there are celery sticks in a plastic bowl, too."

"Don't worry, Mom," I called as she headed down the hall. "I'll take good care of them."

Boy, was that a joke! The instant the front door shut Margo appeared at my door. She was wearing a white bathrobe over her clothes. A toy stethoscope hung from her neck. Claire stood beside her, a white paper hat pinned to her hair.

"Good morning, Miss Pike," Margo said. "I'm Doctor Margolius and this is Nurse Claire."

Claire tugged on Margo's sleeve and whispered into her ear.

"Oh, excuse me," Margo said, straightening up. "I mean, this is Nurse Tiffany." Tiffany was the name Claire happened to like that week.

"How do you do," I said, deciding to play along with them. "Are you two making your rounds?"

Margo looked confused. "Huh?"

"Visiting your patients?" I explained.

"No." Margo shook her head. "You're our only patient."

Claire pointed a pudgy finger at me. "We want you to listen to us 'cause we're in charge."

"It's nearly lunchtime," Margo said. "And in our hospital patients eat at eleven o'clock on the dot."

44

"Lunchtime? I should get you kids something to eat," I said. I flipped back the covers on my bed and started to stand. "Mom said she left some food in the fridge."

"Get back in that bed!" Margo barked. "You're too weak to stand."

"But Margo — I mean, Dr. Margolius, I'm feeling much better. Honest. Besides, Mom asked me to look after you — "

Claire sprang forward and grabbed my wrist. She held onto it and looked at the toy watch she wore on her arm. "Uh-oh. This doesn't look good, doctor," she told Margo.

"Why? Is her pulse too fast?" Margo asked.

Claire shook her head.

"Too slow?"

"No."

Margo put her hands on her hips and asked in exasperation. "*What* then?"

"She doesn't have one."

"That can only mean one thing," Margo said, scribbling furiously on the chart at the foot of my bed.

"What, doctor?" Claire asked wide-eyed.

"She's sick."

"No!" Claire gasped.

"Yes. Very, *very* sick."

Claire leaned her head against the wall. "This is awful."

It took every ounce of my willpower not to

laugh out loud. I decided that Margo and Claire must have been watching too many soap operas, too, because they sounded just like the characters on *Young Doctors in Love*.

"She better eat something fast," Margo declared.

"Right." Claire nodded her head. "Doctor, what should I get?"

Margo rubbed her chin. "I prescribe Animal Crackers, Goofy Grape Kool-Aid, and some M&M's."

I liked that idea. It sounded much better than the Jell-O and chicken soup I had been eating for the past two weeks.

"If you insist, doctor," I said, leaning my head back on my pillow. But then I remembered I was supposed to be taking care of them. And that did not sound like a nutritous lunch. I raised myself on one elbow. "Doctor Margolius and Nurse Tiffany, the hospital had some cheese sandwiches and celery sticks flown in on our MediVac chopper just for you. I believe they're downstairs in the refrigerator."

"Celery sticks?" Claire wrinkled her nose.

"Yes, all the great nurses ate celery sticks," I said solemnly. "Florence Nightingale, Clara Barton, and, uh . . ." (The only other nurse I could think of was from the old TV series M*A*S*H. I told you I was watching too much

TV.) " . . . Hot Lips Hoolihan."

My list seemed to do the trick because Margo and Claire disappeared. When they finally reappeared, they were carrying plates laden with sandwiches and celery sticks. I was relieved. So far I hadn't taken care of them at all. In fact, the way things had been going, they were the baby-sitters and I was the charge.

For the next couple of hours, Claire and Margo took turns reading to me (or in Claire's case, showing me pictures). Every so often one of them would take my temperature or listen to my heart with the stethoscope, but all in all it was a pleasant way to spend the day. I was actually kind of disappointed to see my parents return.

My doctor and nurse were busy taking my pulse for the fifteenth time when my mom popped her head in the door and asked, "How'd it go?"

Margo answered for me. "The patient was a little cranky at first but she took her medicine. Luckily, we didn't have to operate."

"I see." Mom shot me an amused look, then turned to Margo and Claire and said, "All right, you two. I think it's time for your patient to get some rest."

I was still chuckling to myself when I drifted off to sleep.

CHAPTER 6

"I have big news," I announced to my family at the breakfast table on Sunday morning. "I can swallow and it doesn't hurt."

"That's great, honey," Mom said. She squinted at me and shook her head. "Your glands are still a little swollen, though. I can see them from here."

"But I don't have a fever anymore," I said. "Maybe I could go to school tomorrow."

Dad put down his fork. "Mallory, you still don't look well. Now tell the truth. How do you feel?"

"The truth?" I stared at my plate. The truth was, I still felt really tired and dragged out. "A little tired," I murmured.

Mom and Dad exchanged concerned looks and then Mom said, "We need to have a talk after breakfast."

From the tone of her voice, things didn't sound good. And they weren't.

48

"Your recovery has been much slower than we expected," Dad said after the three of us had gone upstairs to my room. I was sitting on one side of my bed, with my parents across from me. "So your mother and I talked to Dr. Dellenkamp."

"What did she say?" I asked in a tiny voice.

"She said that mono hits some people harder than others," Mom replied. "Unfortunately you're one of those people."

Dad cleared his throat. "She said we should keep you home until you get better and then you can go to school, but that's it."

"That's it?" I repeated. "What do you mean."

Dad looked at Mom, who leaned forward and took my hand. "It means no extra activities. No archery team, no school projects, and — "

I closed my eyes and held my breath.

"And no Baby-sitters Club."

I felt as if I'd been punched in the stomach. My voice was quivering when I spoke. "But, Mom, the Baby-sitters Club is one of the most important things in the world to me!"

"I know that. Believe me, this was a very tough decision to make."

Dad sat next to me and put his arm around my shoulders. "We're only thinking of you. Your health comes first."

By now, tears were rolling down my cheeks. "This is terrible," I moaned. "Everyone will think I'm letting them down."

"Mallory, it's not forever," Mom said. "Just until you're back to normal."

"But you don't understand. The BSC needs me. With Dawn gone, we're shorthanded already."

"Maybe they can get a temporary replacement," Dad suggested.

"No!" I cried. "The last person we got was a total disaster. She didn't follow club rules, she took jobs on her own. Luckily she quit, otherwise Kristy would have had to fire her."

I was starting to feel hysterical and I couldn't catch my breath. It was hard enough falling behind in school and missing my friends. How would I live without the BSC?

"I know how much the club means to you, Mallory," Mom said. "But your father's right. We're doing what's best for you."

Deep down inside I knew what Mom was saying was the truth, but it still hurt. A lot.

After my parents left my room, I stared at the phone. There was a call that I had to make but I wasn't looking forward to it.

"Kristy," I said when she answered. "It's me, Mallory."

"Mal! How are you feeling? We really miss you."

I bit my lip and tried to keep a steady voice.

"I miss you, too. Kristy, I have bad news." I had to swallow hard before I could say the next sentence. "Mom and Dad said I have to drop out of the BSC for awhile."

There was a long silence. Finally Kristy murmured, "Mallory, I'm sorry. You must feel terrible."

I nodded, too upset to speak. Finally I said, "Look, Kristy, I can't really talk now, but I just thought you should know so you could start finding a replacement."

After I said good-bye to Kristy, I instantly dialed Jessi.

"You can't quit!" was Jessi's response when I told her my bad news. "The BSC needs you. I need you."

"I need you, too, Jessi, but Mom and Dad won't budge. They say I'm too sick for anything but schoolwork and getting well."

"Oh, Mal," Jessi said. "This is awful." Her voice broke and I knew she was about to cry.

That did it for me. I burst into tears and just sobbed and sobbed.

I must have fallen asleep after my phone calls because the next thing I heard was a knock on my door. Mom ducked her head in and asked softly, "Mallory, are you awake?"

"Hmmm?" I said, drowsily.

"Are you ready to receive guests?"

"I guess so," I said, rubbing my eyes, which were puffy from crying. I sat up in bed and tried to look alert.

Jessi appeared in the doorway. "Oh, Mal!" She ran across the room and we hugged each other. Mom shut the door and left us alone.

"I can't believe it," Jessi said, shaking her head. "I just can't believe it."

"This is the worse thing that has ever happened to me," I said. I could feel my throat start to tighten again.

"Look," Jessi went on, "I can only stay a minute. Kristy has called an emergency BSC meeting. I'm going over to Claudia's now."

I fell back against my pillows. "She probably wants to find a replacement for me right away."

"I don't think that's all she wants to talk about," Jessi said. "But I'll report to you as soon as I can."

"Would you, Jessi?"

"Of course. As soon as it's over, I'll run back here."

"Thanks." I squeezed her hand. "You're a good friend."

After Jessi left I stared at the ceiling trying to imagine what was happening at Claudia's house. Kristy would be sitting in the director's chair, Mary Anne would be cross-legged on

52

the bed, Stacey and Claudia would be beside her, and Jessi would be on the floor in front of the bed. Next to her would be an empty place. Mine.

"The emergency meeting of the Baby-sitters Club is called to order," Kristy would announce. "I've got some really bad news. Mallory has to quit the club."

Everyone would be shocked and then Claudia would probably say, "We're dropping like flies. First Dawn, and now Mallory."

"We need to act on this right away," Kristy would say.

I closed my eyes and murmured, "And then they'll replace me."

It was hard to imagine my life without the BSC. No more meetings. No more baby-sitting, or talent shows, or backyard circuses, or group hikes. No more pizza parties. No more fun.

I pointed the remote control at the TV and numbly flipped through the channels. "Sports. Nothing but sports. Doesn't anybody watch anything but football and golf on Sundays?"

After I'd circled the channels a few times, I tried to do some homework. It was too hard to concentrate. All I could think about was the BSC meeting. Luckily for me, Jessi appeared before I completely lost my mind.

She was smiling when she came in. "First of all, everyone says hi," she announced as she sat on the foot of my bed.

"Who's everyone?"

"Everyone else in the BSC, including Logan and Shannon."

"I'm surprised they all made it to the meeting on such short notice."

"This was very important. Claudia skipped an art class, and Logan missed football practice."

"Wow." I was impressed.

"Okay. Here's how it went." Jessi settled herself comfortably on the bed. "First Kristy called the meeting to order and broke the news."

"Was everybody shocked?"

"And terribly upset. They all said it was unfair of your parents to make you quit. Claud wanted to write your parents a letter of protest and have us all sign it."

"You mean, a petition?" I asked with a laugh.

Jessi grinned. "Then Logan suggested we make signs and march around in front of your house, shouting things like 'Unfair!' and 'Free Mallory!' "

I fell back against my pillow, giggling.

"But it was Mary Anne who said we should accept your parents' decision as long as it was just temporary. So we took a vote."

"And?"

"It was unanimous. Nobody wants to replace you."

"Really?"

"You're too valuable a member to lose. We decided just to muddle through the best we can until you're well again."

"Oh, Jessi!"

Jessi squeezed my hand. "That's when Kristy suggested we name you an honorary BSC member until you return."

"An honorary member." I tried out the words and then beamed at Jessi. "I like it."

Jessi stood up. "And as honorary member, it is your duty to get well soon. Understand?"

I saluted her. "Yes, ma'am."

Jessi grinned at me. Then she walked to the bedroom door. Just before she left she turned and said softly, "I'm really glad we aren't going to replace you."

"Me, too," I replied with a smile.

Jessi shut the door and I sank happily back into my pillows. Pulling my quilt up to my chin, I murmured once again, "Me, too."

CHAPTER 7

On Monday I was still feeling numb from my parents' announcement. I sat on the couch downstairs and watched my brothers and sisters get ready for school. The moment when everyone is actually supposed to leave is usually pretty zooey and today was no exception.

"Where's my homework?" Byron bellowed, rifling through the backpacks by the front door. He held up a blue notebook.

"That's mine," Adam protested. "Give it back."

"I can't find my boot," Nicky wailed.

"My hair looks terrible," Vanessa grumbled as she stood in front of the hall mirror, struggling with a comb. "There's a knot in it. I can't go to school with a knot in my hair."

"Mom, I hope you didn't make tuna sandwiches again," Margo said. "I'm getting sick of tuna."

Mom stood at the front door in her bathrobe

with six bag lunches in her hands (Claire is always at home for lunch because kindergarten is only a half day). Her voice was very calm as she said, "Byron, your homework is in the den where you left it. Nicky, your other boot is in the front closet and, no, Margo, you're not getting tuna. Today is ham-and-cheese day." Then she turned to Vanessa. "If you'll wait half a second, I'll brush your hair."

When the kids had left, Mom shut the door and sighed. "Another week has begun."

I would have laughed but I was suddenly hit with a case of the blues. Another week had begun but nothing had changed. I was still in my pajamas, still just lying on the couch, and still feeling lousy.

I thought about all the things that were happening at school. Thanksgiving was only a few weeks away and the halls were probably covered with pictures of turkeys and Pilgrims and cornucopias. Skits were being rehearsed in most of the classrooms. And kids were already making plans to get together over the holiday.

"At least we still have our New York trip," I murmured. "That's something to look forward to."

Mom had gone into the kitchen to clean up the rest of the breakfast dishes and heard me muttering to myself. "Did you want something, Mallory?" she asked.

"Yes," I moaned. "I want to get well."

Mom sat beside me on the couch and smoothed her hand over my forehead. "Being sick is no fun," she said. "I know."

"I just wish there was some pill or medicine I could take that would make me better."

"Maybe there is something," Mom said. "We'll ask Dr. Dellenkamp. You have an appointment with her this morning."

"I do?" I sat up, excited. "I'll go get dressed right now."

This may sound stupid, but I'd spent so much time lying around the house that the thought of actually getting dressed and going somewhere was thrilling. Even if the somewhere was just the doctor's office, I didn't care. At least I was getting out.

An hour later Mom and I were in the car. I savored every minute of the drive. "Look, Mom, the grocery store has turkeys on sale. And look over at the drugstore. They've got a scarecrow in the window with all those little pumpkins. Isn't that cute?"

Mom looked at me sideways. "Boy, you really are going stir crazy."

We didn't have to wait long at Dr. Dellenkamp's, which was kind of disappointing. When I'm there I like to read all those magazines that Mom never buys.) The nurse weighed me and I'd lost five pounds. (Not good. My jeans were starting to look really baggy.) Then she took me to an examining room, where she checked my blood pressure and took my temperature. Dr. Dellenkamp and my mom came in a few minutes later.

"Your mother tells me you're not enjoying being cooped up at home." Dr. Dellenkamp felt the glands in my neck and under my arms and listened to my heart while she talked.

"I hate it," I said matter-of-factly.

"I don't blame you." Dr. Dellenkamp tucked her stethoscope back in her pocket. "Unfortunately, with mono, the only cure is bed rest."

"But for how long?" I asked. "I feel like I've been in bed forever."

Dr. Dellenkamp pursed her lips and looked at Mom. "In some cases, a full recovery can take as long as three months."

"Three months!" I gasped. "But that's terrible. I'll miss December and January."

"It might even stretch into February."

"I'll miss so much school they'll flunk me!"

"Now, don't panic," Dr. Dellenkamp said in her best comforting voice (which wasn't very comforting). "You're a good student. As long as you keep up with your homework, no one will think about holding you back. And if you do get too far behind, there's always summer school."

"Summer school?" My chin was starting to quiver. First I was being told that I might not be able to do anything for half the school year. Then they were telling me I might miss summer vacation. I looked at Mom and stammered, "T-t-tell her I can't. I won't."

Mom put her arm around my shoulder. "Dr. Dellenkamp didn't say you had to go to summer school. She's just trying to let you know that this is not as terrible as you may think."

Dr. Dellenkamp nodded. "Your progress is going slowly, but that doesn't mean it will always be that way. You may see a real improvement in a few weeks. We'll just have to take this one day at a time."

Things seemed to be going from bad to worse. I looked out the window as we drove home but this time I didn't notice anything. My eyes were too blurred with tears.

The one bright spot in my day was Jessi's visit. She stopped by before the BSC meeting. I told her my news.

"So who knows when my parents will let me baby-sit again," I said finally. "Probably never."

"You're just feeling depressed," Jessi said gently. "They'll let you baby-sit again. And until they do, you don't have to worry. The BSC won't replace you."

"That's really nice," I said. "But what if I

am sick for three months, like Dr. Dellenkamp said? You guys will be working yourselves to the bone, trying to keep up with my sitting jobs."

"Relax," Jessi said. "We can handle it."

I was beginning to feel that I wasn't being fair to the rest of the club. Maybe they *should* replace me. I decided not to talk about it. Instead, I switched the subject.

"How's the Thanksgiving project coming?" I asked.

"We're definitely going to put together those baskets for Stoneybrook Manor but we haven't decided how we're going to raise the money for the food and supplies. We better think of something soon. Thanksgiving is only two weeks away."

"A Saturday car wash might be a good fundraiser," I suggested. "People probably want their cars to look nice for the holiday."

Jessi pulled a pad of paper out of her bookbag and wrote down the idea. "We could bake cookies and sell them at the car wash," she added.

"We could also ask people to donate money to sponsor a basket. Then we could put their names in the basket."

"Good idea!" Jessi said. "We could include cards that say, 'To Mr. Jones from Mr. or Ms. Whomever and the BSC.' "

I gestured to my bedroom. "I'm stuck in here so I'm not much good at a car wash, but I could make phone calls and look for sponsors."

"That would be a big help," said Jessi, sounding relieved. "Now that we're two baby-sitters short, no one has very much spare time."

I know Jessi didn't mean to hurt me, but her words just underlined my fear that the BSC members were now working too hard because of me.

"If we do decide on a bake sale," Jessi added, "you could also make cookies."

"If Mom will let me. She and Dad barely let me do anything." I winced. "They may not even let me make phone calls."

Jessi patted my shoulder. "You talk to your parents and I'll talk to the BSC. In the meantime, we also have to think of what we could do when we present our baskets at Stoneybrook Manor."

"You mean, put on a Thanksgiving skit or something?"

Jessi shook her head. "Kristy said the people there see skits all the time. She wants us to think of something else. Something more unusual."

I scratched my head. "That'll take some thinking." Then I laughed for the first time since Jessi arrived. "Time is the one thing I have plenty of."

Jessi checked her wristwatch. "Oops. Not me. I better run. The meeting starts in ten minutes. Write down any other ideas you come up with and call me later. I'll tell everyone about the car wash and sponsors."

"Be sure and let them know I'm ready and willing to make calls for the fundraiser."

"They'll be glad to hear that." Jessi gave me a hug. "See? You may be stuck in bed, but as an honorary member you're doing everybody a lot of good."

I tried to feel encouraged, but deep down inside I didn't. Jessi's words kept running over and over in my head: "Now that we're two baby-sitters short, nobody has any spare time."

CHAPTER 8

Tuesday

Sitting for the Barretts
is always an adventure.
Today was no different.
At the Monday BSC
meeting, Kristy had
suggested we call
kids in our neighborhood
and tell them about
a big planning meeting
at Mary Anne's the
next day. I was
scheduled to sit for
the Barretts on Tuesday
so when I called to find
out if it was all
right to bring them to
the meeting, Buddy was
ecstatic. Not about the
meeting, but about

where it was going to be held. In Mary Anne's barn!

Most of the BSC members had already arrived at Mary Anne's when Jessi showed up with Buddy, Marnie, and Suzi Barrett. Stacey and Charlotte Johanssen were busy chatting in one corner of the barn with Mary Anne and the Arnold twins. Logan had offered to bring along my brothers, who were playing hide-and-seek in the horse stalls. Becca and Margo and Claire had come with Claudia, who was showing them the door to the secret passage leading to Mary Anne's house.

"Oh, boy!" Buddy cried as Jessi and the Barrett kids walked through the big red barn doors. "Let's go jump in the hay!"

Before Jessi could say, "Wait a minute," Buddy had run for the nearest mound of hay and hurled himself at it.

"Ouch!" a voice cried from under Buddy. "What's the big idea?"

Buddy scrambled for the side of the stall. "Something's in there!" he gasped, wide-eyed.

"I think you mean some*one*," Jessi replied with a laugh. "That'll teach you to leap before you look."

Nicky stuck his head out of the straw and looked around. "Who jumped on my head?"

"I did!" Buddy said, bending his knees. "Want me to do it again?"

"Oh, no, you don't!" Jessi cried, catching Buddy's arm. "This is a meeting, not a free-for-all."

"EEEEEK!" a voice squealed from the far side of the barn. It was Charlotte Johanssen. "I saw a mouse."

In a flash every kid had raced to Charlotte's corner.

"Where?" Byron demanded.

"Under the hay." Charlotte pointed to a metal feeding trough by one of the stalls. "It was icky with red beady eyes."

"Maybe it was a rat!" Jordan announced with glee. That set off a round of shrieks from Becca and the Arnold twins.

Before things got too out of hand, Mary Anne said firmly, "It's not a rat. It's just a little tiny field mouse that's hungry and came into the barn."

Becca looked less disgusted. "Poor little mouse," she murmured. "Let's get it something to eat."

Kristy arrived just then. She had brought David Michael, Karen, and the Korman kids with her.

"Hi, everybody!" Kristy called. "Are you

ready to put on your thinking caps?"

"Yes!" Buddy bellowed.

Jessi could only shrug. "At least he's enthusiastic," she said, laughing.

The next few minutes were spent arranging bales of hay in a semi-circle and directing everyone to sit on them. Jessi sat with two-year-old Marnie Barrett in her lap and five-year-old Suzi at her side. Nicky and Buddy squeezed in between Jessi and Logan.

"I'd like to welcome you all to the first official meeting of the Thanksgiving Project," Kristy said, stepping onto an old milk crate in front of the group of kids. "This is really an exciting project. Our hope is to bring a lot of happiness to the people at Stoneybrook Manor."

"My dad's Uncle Joe lives there," Nicky spoke up.

"That's right." Kristy smiled. "And we're going to visit him in less than two weeks. We'd like to bring goody baskets with us."

"What kinds of goodies?" Marilyn Arnold asked.

"We thought we'd put in fruit and maybe some chocolates, but we can put in other things. Do you guys have any suggestions?"

"You could give them presents," Melody Korman said.

"Trucks and dinosaurs!" Buddy shouted.

Kristy listened while Mary Anne wrote down everything in a notebook.

"How about pictures?" Carolyn Arnold suggested. "We just got our school pictures back and we have a ton left over."

Bill Korman scratched his head. "Hey, if we gave them our pictures, we could make frames for them."

"Out of construction paper?" David Michael asked.

Bill shook his head. "No. We'd build them out of wood."

Charlotte whispered an idea to Stacey (I guess she's still a little shy in groups). "Charlotte thinks we should put in books since they probably have a lot of time to read," Stacey said.

"Paperback books aren't too expensive. We could even get them at a used bookstore," Jessi suggested.

"And for those who can't see well, we should buy books on tape," Mary Anne added.

Kristy nodded. "That brings me to the subject of fundraising. We need to earn enough money to buy these books and tapes and fruits and candies. Mallory suggested we hold a car wash. How many of you would be interested in working on that?"

All of the kids raised their hands (even Marnie, who had been busy sticking bits of straw in her hair).

The idea of squirting cars with a hose sounded awfully appealing to Buddy. "Could we wear our bathing suits?"

"In November?" Mary Anne gasped. "You'd freeze."

Claudia nodded. "Mary Anne's got a point. Maybe a car wash isn't such a great idea. You could all come down with pneumonia."

Kristy tugged on the bill of her baseball cap. "If we don't have a car wash, then we'd better come up with something else. It'll probably cost a lot of money to put together these baskets."

"I'll donate my allowance," Karen offered.

"Me too!" Nicky and Margo agreed.

"Me three," said Buddy.

Suddenly all the kids were talking about pooling their money.

Mary Anne looked as if she were about to cry. "Oh, you guys," she said. "This is so sweet."

"You know, we do have some money in the club treasury," Stacey said. "It's not a lot, but if we combined it with the kids' allowances, and then kicked in a little extra from our baby-sitting jobs, we might have enough to buy some things."

"Mallory suggested we get sponsors for the

baskets," Jessie added. "We could start by asking our parents and clients if they'd like to become a sponsor."

"How much would it cost to be one?" Logan asked.

Jessi shrugged. "How does five dollars sound?"

Kristy consulted her clipboard. "There are fifty-five residents at Stoneybrook Manor. I wonder if we can come up with that many sponsors."

Claire shook her head. "I don't even know fifty-five people."

"If a grocery store donated the fruit and candy, or at least gave us a discount," Logan suggested, "then the baskets wouldn't cost so much."

"Cool!" Stacey said. "Why doesn't every member of the BSC talk to a grocery store, then report in on Monday?"

"Good suggestion," Kristy said. "Which brings me to the last piece of business. Our program."

"Do we have to dress up like turkeys?" Buddy asked. "My school is making me dress up like a turkey and I hate it."

"No." Kristy laughed. "We don't have to dress up like turkeys. But we should do something fun."

"Playing games is fun," Suzi exclaimed. "And carnivals are fun."

Buddy turned to his sister and rolled his eyes. "Old people don't want to play games or go to carnivals."

"Why not?" Suzi asked.

"Because . . . well, because they're old," Buddy replied.

Mary Anne sat up straight. "You know what? I think Suzi has come up with a brilliant idea. Why not put together a Thanksgiving funhouse?"

"What do you mean?" Kristy asked. "Like a haunted house?"

Mary Anne shook her head. "More like the carnival Suzi was talking about. Every year the people at Stoneybrook Manor sit in chairs and watch groups of people parade in and out, singing songs or doing skits for them. But do they ever get to do anything themselves? No."

Kristy's eyes widened. "I get it. We set up a carnival with booths, and let them have fun."

"We can have a cakewalk, and a bean bag throw," Mary Anne continued.

"A softball throw," Kristy added.

"A fishing booth," Byron said. "I've always liked that one."

Logan snapped his fingers. "Everything

could have a Thanksgiving theme. Like, throw-the-beanbag-in-the-Pilgrim's-mouth. And pin-the-feather-on-the-turkey."

Charlotte turned to Stacey and giggled. "This sounds like fun."

"We could make the booths right here," Mary Anne said, "in our barn. In fact, we could start tomorrow."

Logan leaned over Mary Anne's shoulder. "Put me down to head the work crew."

"Now, then." Kristy scratched her head. "What would we give as prizes?"

Suzi Barrett thrust her hand in the air. "Cookies."

"I'll be in charge of the baking," Claudia said. "We could make pumpkin- and turkey-shaped cookies, and decorate them."

Kristy flopped down on the milk crate and stared out at the group of kids. "Phew. Baking, building carnival booths, raising money, and decorating baskets — that's a lot of work. We only have twelve days. Can we do it?"

There was a moment of silence. Then a huge cheer echoed through the barn. "Yes! Yes! Yes!"

After the official meeting ended, the chatter continued. The kids vowed to do extra clean-up jobs to earn more allowance. Bill Korman swore that not only would his parents be sponsors, so would both sets of grandparents.

"Let's see, that's six times five . . ." Bill did the multiplication in his head, then looked up happily and announced to the barn in general, "That's thirty dollars just from my family alone!"

While the kids talked, Jessi pulled a sheet of paper from her notebook and hurriedly wrote the following note:

Mal, I know you're feeling kind of useless right now. Here's a list of things you can do that would really help the Thanksgiving Project:

1. *Make calls to find sponsors*
2. *Bake cookies*
3. *Make bean bags for the bag toss*
4. *Gift wrap books for the goody baskets*
5. *(Most important!) Get well soon!*

Call me!
Love Jessi

Claudia had gathered Becca, Margo, and Vanessa together and was just leaving the barn when Jessi stopped them.

"Margo, wait up!" Jessi cried, waving her

note in the air. "Can you please give this to Mallory?"

Margo held out her hand. "What is it?"

"It's a list of ways Mallory can help our project without ever leaving her bed."

"I'll be sure and give it to her," Margo said, carefully tucking the note in her coat pocket. "I promise."

Jessi thanked her, then turned to look for the Barrett kids. Buddy was perched on the ladder leading to the hayloft, clutching a rope that hung from a hook in the rafters.

"Watch this, Jessi," he called merrily. "I'm Tarzan."

"I'm the baby-sitter!" Jessi shouted back. "And I say let go of that rope before I have a heart attack."

Buddy let go reluctantly. "Aw, Jessi," he grumbled. "I never get to have any fun."

Jessi helped him down the ladder, then scooped Marnie up in one arm and took Suzi's hand with the other. "Come on. Why don't we play follow-the-leader on the way home? Buddy, you can be the leader."

"All right!" Buddy squatted down in front of Jessi and the girls. "The leader says, hop like a frog!"

Jessi winced. "Oh, boy."

The four of them hopped the entire way back to the Barrett house.

CHAPTER 9

While everybody was meeting at Mary Anne's barn, I lay in bed worrying about the BSC. Kristy and the others were already feeling the strain of having to take extra sitting jobs. How would they feel in two months? They'd probably hate me. I just couldn't let that happen. And I knew if I tried to quit, they wouldn't let me. So the only way to remain friends with everyone was to get them to kick me out of the club so they could replace me. But how?

Before I could think of a solution, Claudia appeared at my bedroom door with Margo and Claire. "Hi, Mal," she said. "We're back from Mary Anne's."

"How did it go?" I asked.

Claud sat on a chair across the room from me. "It was better than anybody expected. We had a million great suggestions, and now we have a million projects to finish in twelve days."

"We're going to give a Thanksgiving Carnival for the old people," Claire announced as she climbed onto my bed. "So they can have fun."

"With games and prizes for everybody," Margo added.

"What about the goody baskets?" I asked.

"We're doing those, too," Claudia said. "And we're trying to raise money to pay for everything."

"Wow," I exclaimed. "That *is* a lot of stuff to do."

"Oh," Margo said. "I almost forgot." She pulled a piece of paper out of her pocket and handed it to me. "This is from Jessi. It's a list of things you can do for the Thanksgiving Project."

"Oh?" As I stared at Jessi's list, I realized that this was my opportunity to show the BSC the mistake they'd made by keeping me in the club. It took every ounce of willpower I could muster to do it.

First I frowned. Then I tossed the note at my bedside table. "Maybe I don't feel like doing anything. I am sick, you know," I said in a grumpy voice.

Claudia's eyes widened in surprise. "Wow, Mallory, we know you're sick. But I think Jessi had the impression that you wanted to help on this project."

I shrugged and, flopping my head back on my pillows, stared at the ceiling. "Maybe I do and maybe I don't."

I couldn't see Claudia or Margo, but I could tell by their silence that they were shooting each other I-don't-understand looks. My plan was working.

Finally Claudia cleared her throat. "Well, I guess I should let you get some sleep," she said, standing up.

"Thanks," I murmured. "I do feel pretty tired." Then I added, "Tell Jessi I'll try to find time to look at her list later."

"Yeah. Sure," Claudia said, backing out of the room. "But if you can't, don't worry about it. See you later."

Margo and Claire escorted her to the front door. After everyone had left my room, I heaved a huge sigh of relief. It was hard being so hateful. Every part of me wanted to shout, "I'm just kidding. I really want to help!" But I knew that what I was doing was for the best.

I reached for Jessi's note but before I had a chance to look at it, Margo was back at my door.

"Boy, Mallory, you really were mean to Claudia."

"I wasn't mean," I said, crossing my fingers

under the covers. "I was just being honest."

"We need people to make phone calls to grocery store owners."

"So?"

"So that's something you could do. You're just lying around in bed."

"The doctor and Mom and Dad told me to cut out all extra activities. That is definitely an extra activity."

"Boy, oh, boy," Margo said, shaking her head sadly. "I thought you were a nice person."

"Well, you thought wrong." I rolled over and faced the wall because I couldn't bear looking at the hurt on Margo's face. Getting kicked out of the club was going to be harder on me than I had thought.

On Sunday, Jessi dropped by for a visit. She was carrying two videotapes and an armload of horse books that she'd gotten for me at the library. "Here, I thought you needed some entertainment. If you're too tired to read then you can watch *The Black Stallion* or *National Velvet*." (Two of my favorite movies.)

"Thanks, Jessi," I said, eagerly reaching for the books and movies. "That's really thoughtful."

"Did you get my list for the Thanksgiving project?" she asked.

I guessed she hadn't talked to Claudia or Margo.

"Yeah. I looked at it," I said.

"What do you think? I wrote down a lot of things you'd be able to do that would really help us out."

"Well . . ." I took a long, long pause. It's hard to act like a jerk with your best friend. Especially when she just brought you presents. "Can't you make those phone calls?"

"Sure," Jessi replied. "But I thought you'd want to do it."

"It's not that I don't want to," I said, getting ready to tell a big fib. "It's just that Claudia told me you would handle the list."

"She said I would handle it?" Jessi repeated, confused. "I'm not sure what you mean."

I slumped down under my covers. I couldn't bear to look Jessi in the eye. "Maybe Claud thinks you're not doing enough."

Jessi stood up indignantly. "I'm doing plenty. Right now I'm going to Logan's work session to help build the carnival booths, and I've already baked two dozen cookies."

"Maybe Claudia just wants to take over," I added. "And doesn't like the idea of you handing out assignments."

Jessi bit her lip thoughtfully. Then she frowned at me. "I doubt it," she said, "but I'll talk to her today and see what's going on."

I was relieved when Jessi left. Acting like a jerk was hard work. I decided not to answer the phone for the rest of the day. That way I wouldn't have to deal with anyone.

Sunday and Monday dragged by endlessly. On Tuesday night, Mom came into my room. "Mallory, I have a list of phone messages for you that's a whole page long. Haven't you been getting them?"

"Yes, I got them," I said. "I just haven't felt like calling anybody back."

Mom smoothed her hand over my forehead. "I know you feel cut off from school and baby-sitting, but you shouldn't shut out your friends. They want to help."

I didn't feel like arguing with Mom, so I agreed to make an effort to return the calls. Then Mom stood up and said, "I hope you don't mind, but you have some visitors."

"Here? Now? But I look terrible." I hadn't combed my hair in two days.

"It's okay," Mom said. "They're friends. They'll understand."

Kristy and Mary Anne peeked around the door. It was great to see their smiling faces. I was all ready to smile back, but then I remembered my plan.

"Oh," I said in a dull voice. "It's just you."

Mary Anne looked a little hurt but Kristy marched into the room and gave me a hug. "Hi, Mal. How are you feeling?"

I shrugged. "So-so."

Kristy pulled a piece of paper out of the back pocket of her jeans. "First, I'm supposed to tell you that everyone misses you."

"Oh, really?" I replied. "I've been so busy with my homework that I haven't had a chance to miss anyone myself."

Mary Anne was hanging back by the door. "It's good that you've kept busy," she said softly. "There's nothing worse than lying in bed. Some people get very depressed."

I wanted to agree with Mary Anne and tell her that I'd never felt so down in my life. That the days felt endless, and I spent the nights tossing and turning because I'd slept too much during the day. Instead I said, "What do I have to be depressed about? I don't have to go to school and that suits me just fine."

Kristy blinked several times in surprise. It's no secret that I like school and hate to miss even half a day. "Boy, Mal, having mono has really changed you," she said.

Mary Anne shifted her weight uncomfortably. "Kristy, maybe we should talk to Mal about the project."

"Oh, right." Kristy consulted her list again. "Jessi and Claud said you were given a list of things to do. Have you been able to arrange for any sponsors?"

I shook my head. "No."

"Did you make any bean bags?"

I shook my head again. "Uh-uh."

"How about cookies?" Mary Anne asked. "Were you able to bake any?"

"Nope."

Finally Kristy said, "Have you done *any* work on the project?"

"No." I took a sip of juice from the glass on my night stand. "I've just been too busy. Okay?"

"Gee, Mallory," Mary Anne said, "you sound kind of angry. We didn't mean to make you mad. We just hoped that you'd be able to help us out."

"I can't help anybody but myself," I replied, folding my arms across my chest. "So go find someone else to do your errands."

If I had any doubts about the success of my plan, they were gone. My bad attitude had definitely upset Kristy. And Mary Anne looked as if she were about to burst into tears.

"Kristy," Mary Anne murmured, "I think we should leave."

"Right." Kristy stood up stiffly. Then she said in a very cold, very final voice, "We won't bother you anymore."

As I watched them leave, two tears rolled down my cheeks. My plan had worked. Soon I'd be getting a call telling me that I wasn't needed in the club and would be replaced, and it would be all over.

I'd never go to another BSC meeting. I'd probably never see any of the members again. And Jessi, who was my best friend in the whole world, would stop calling me too. I wanted to bury my head under the covers and stay there. Forever.

I managed to stay in bed for the rest of the night and all the next day. In fact, my lack of enthusiasm about everything was starting to worry my parents. I heard them murmuring outside my bedroom door Friday morning and again Friday afternoon. But I didn't care. I just wanted to be left alone in my misery.

Ring ring.

I was sitting in bed reading when the phone startled me. I looked at the clock. Five forty-five.

Ring ring.

I wasn't about to answer. I was sure it wasn't for me. I didn't have any friends. Not anymore. I went back to my book.

Ring ring.

Adam stuck his head in my room. "The phone's ringing," he said.

"I know," I answered, not looking up from the page.

Adam dashed into the room, picked up the phone, and said, "Pikes' Place," Then he handed the receiver to me. "It's for you."

I sighed heavily and said, "Hello?"

"Mallory, it's Jessi."

Before I could say anything, more voices came on the line. "And Kristy."

"And Claudia — "

"And Mary Anne — "

"And Stacey — "

"And Logan."

Jessi's voice came back on the line. "We're calling you from the meeting at Claudia's."

"Oh." This was it. They'd probably just voted to kick me out of the club, permanently. I gritted my teeth and waited for the bad news.

"Mal," Jessi said sternly. "We know what you're doing and it won't work."

This took me totally by surprise. "What do you mean?"

Kristy took the phone. "We've just spent an incredible fifteen minutes arguing with each other over things *you* said."

Then it was Claudia's turn. "Jessi and I were getting really miffed with each other before we figured out that *you* had started *our* fight by inventing stories about me."

Jessi took the phone back. "Then we realized that everything you've said and done lately was completely unlike you."

I could hear Mary Anne speaking over Jessi's shoulder. "We decided you were trying to make us angry with you so we'd kick you out of the club."

Kristy took the phone. "And you did a pretty good job of it, too. I was ready to replace you."

My voice sounded awfully tiny when I asked, "Why didn't you?"

A chorus of voices answered me. "Because we love you!"

Stacey came on the line. "And no matter how sick you get, you can't get rid of us."

A huge lump formed in my throat. I felt frustrated and happy all at once. "Oh, you guys . . ." was all I could manage to say before I burst into tears.

After I blew my nose, and took several sips of water, I finally was able to talk. "I'm sorry. I hope I didn't hurt anybody too badly. I was just trying — "

"You were trying to help us out by leaving," Kristy finished for me. "But we need you to stay."

"Really?"

"Really. The fact of the matter is that Thanksgiving is less than a week away and we need you to help man the phones for our project. Would you do that, Mal? Please?"

I smiled for the first time in at least five days.

"You can count on me!"

CHAPTER 10

Friday evening I lay on my bed in my clothes — *not* my pajamas. I had changed into a pair of jeans and a sweat shirt and felt like a human being once more. It's amazing how a phone call from your friends can change your outlook on life. I still felt dragged out but I was happy.

I flipped to a new page in my journal and made a list of the things Kristy told me had to be done for the Thanksgiving Project by next Tuesday. I wrote:

1. Collect all money by Saturday
2. Go shopping Saturday afternoon
3. Assemble goody baskets Sunday
4. Finish making carnival booths on Monday
5. Go to Stoneybrook Manor after school on Tuesday

"Phew," I said, as I set down my pen. "That's a lot of work. We'd better get cracking."

After dinner that night I sent an announcement to my family. "I'm holding a meeting of all of the Pike kids in my room, right now."

Minutes later my brothers and sisters were sitting on the floor in a half circle around my bed.

"Okay," I began, opening my journal, "how much money do you still need to raise so Kristy can go shopping tomorrow afternoon?"

Vanessa tilted her head. "Well, I heard today that we were short about a hundred dollars."

"A hundred!" I gasped. "That's a lot!"

Margo slumped against the bed. "We'll never raise that much money," she groaned.

"Not by tomorrow," Byron said.

"Yeah, it's hopeless," Adam added.

"Now just a minute." I held up my hands for silence. "There are a lot of kids involved in this project, right?"

Jordan nodded. "I think there are about twenty of us, plus the Baby-sitters Club members."

I made some quick mental calculations and said, "That works out to about three dollars and fifty cents per person. That's not so terrible."

"It is if you don't have even one dollar," Nicky muttered.

"What have you already done to raise money?" I asked the group.

"I emptied my piggy bank," Margo said.

"Me too," Claire added.

"And all of the kids on the project donated this week's allowance," Vanessa said.

"I found two quarters and five pennies under the couch cushions," Nicky said. "And Buddy Barrett found a whole dollar in his couch."

"Claudia suggested that everybody search their coat pockets, so we did," Adam said. "I came up with almost two dollars."

"My teacher gave a dollar," Vanessa said. "And Mom and Dad gave five dollars."

"Most of the kids have asked their parents to sponsor baskets," Byron said, "and Bill and Melody Korman even got advances on their allowances."

"Yikes," I muttered. "You guys have done quite a bit. What's left?"

"Promises," replied Vanessa.

"Excuse me?" I said.

"Promises," she repeated, raising up on her knees and resting her elbows on my bed. "We could promise Mom and Dad — or other people — that we'll do jobs for them, like rake leaves or wash their car. Then they pay us for them now and we do the work later."

"You mean, like those car commercials?"

Jordan joked. "You know, the ones that tell you to buy now and pay later?"

Vanessa nodded. "Exactly."

I tossed my pen in the air and squealed, "Excellent!"

My outburst was so startling that Nicky and Margo shrieked. "What? What's excellent?"

"The promises campaign." I hopped off the bed and wrapped my arms around my sister. "Vanessa, you're a genius!"

Her cheeks flushed a deep pink. "Well, I wouldn't say that . . ." she started to murmur but I didn't let her finish. I was too excited. I paced back and forth across the room in front of my brothers and sisters, thinking out loud.

"All this would involve is lots of phone calls." Suddenly I stopped. "What time is it?"

Claire held up her Mickey Mouse wristwatch. "It's thirty o'clock."

Adam tried to read the watch over her shoulder. "I think she means it's seven-thirty," he declared.

"Hmmmm." I tapped my lips with my finger. "That gives me about two hours to make calls. You guys go work on Mom and Dad."

"What do we say?" Nicky asked.

"Tell them you'd like to sell them a promise, and then offer to do a chore next week," Vanessa replied.

At that moment, Dad walked past my bedroom and down the hall. Nicky raced to the door. "Dad, wait! I have to promise you something."

"Promise me what?" he asked.

Nicky thought fast. "Uh . . . I promise not to play with your golf clubs if you'll give me a quarter."

"That's not the way it works," Adam said, stepping in front of Nicky. "Dad, I promise to polish your shoes and clean out the inside of the car if you'll give me a dollar."

"A dollar? For all of that?" Dad said with a smile. "It's a deal."

Nicky put his hands on his hips. "My offer was better and would've cost you a lot less."

Dad reached into his pocket for change. "Tell you what. I'll take both of your offers."

That did it. Suddenly Dad was swarmed by seven kids all promising to do him a favor — for a fee.

I was giggling when I made my first phone call.

"Jessi, it's Mal. I've got the most wonderful idea. Well, actually, it's not my idea, it's Vanessa's."

I told Jessi about the promise campaign. Her reaction was just like mine.

"That's excellent! I think I'll promise to make breakfast for a week. Mom would love that. And Becca can promise to help fold laundry. That's her favorite chore."

"My brothers and sisters are selling Mom and Dad every promise they can think of," I added. "And I just heard Adam say he was going to run next door and promise to rake leaves for the neighbors."

Jessi chuckled. "Seven Pikes selling promises could make a big dent in a hundred dollars."

"I hope so."

"What else can I do to help?" Jessi asked.

"Well, I think I can call most of the kids on the project, but I don't know if I'll have time to call Kristy and Claud and everyone and tell them what we're up to. Would you mind doing that?"

"Of course not," Jessi replied. "What are friends for?"

"Thanks, Jessi," I said warmly. "I'm glad you don't hate me for being so rotten all week."

"Of course I don't hate you." There was a long pause and then Jessi added, "But don't let it happen again."

"Yes, ma'am!" I cried. "Now let's get going. We've got to raise a hundred dollars by tomorrow morning!"

I spent the next two hours furiously dialing all of the kids on the Thanksgiving project, and every client and friend of my parents that

I knew. This may sound silly but my ear ached from being on the phone for so long. And my index finger was sore from punching so many buttons. But it was worth it. On Saturday morning, Kristy called with the good news.

"Mal, you did it!" Kristy's voice rang in my ear. "Your promise campaign raised over a hundred dollars."

"You're kidding!" I gasped.

"Here, I'll let Stacey give you the exact details."

I heard a lot of shuffling and giggling and then Stacey got on the phone. "Mal, kids have been calling here all morning. According to my calculations, we raised one hundred and forty-two dollars and fifty cents."

I heard some other voices murmur in the background and Stacey said, "No, wait a minute, make that fifty-three cents. Buddy found some more pennies in his couch."

"Stacey, this is great news," I said. "You guys must be really proud."

"You're the one who should be proud. If you hadn't made those calls, we never would have done it."

I can't tell you how great I felt. I hopped out of bed and ran to the top of the stairs.

"Mom! Dad! Everybody!" I shouted. "Come quick!"

Mom and Margo were still clearing the

breakfast dishes. They hurried out of the kitchen to the foot of the stairs. The triplets peeked out of the living room and Dad, who was trying to fix the bathroom sink, ran into the foyer with a wrench in his hand.

"Mallory, are you all right?" he called anxiously. "Is something wrong?"

"No, Dad." I giggled. "For once, something is right!"

My family stared at me, waiting for my announcement.

"We did it!" I cried. "We needed to raise a hundred dollars overnight. So I made about a jillion calls, telling everyone about Vanessa's promise campaign — and we did it!"

"Oh, Mallory," Mom said, hurrying up the stairs, "that's wonderful."

"You bet it is," I said as Mom wrapped her arms around me in a big hug. "We'll have our program at Stoneybrook Manor. Then on Wednesday morning, we'll head for New York to celebrate."

The smile faded from Mom's face and she glanced nervously down at Dad. "Mallory, about New York . . ."

I suddenly got this topsy-turvy feeling in my stomach. I asked quietly, "We're going, aren't we?"

"Well — "

"We found a hotel. The reservations are all

made, and we have those parade tickets. We *have* to go!"

Dad set the wrench on the table in the foyer and joined Mom on the stairs. "Mallory, your mother and I have talked about this," he said slowly. "And we just don't think it's a good idea for you to go to New York."

"But why? I feel a hundred times better than I did even two days ago."

"That's just the point. You're *finally* recovering."

"The doctor's concerned that all the activity and excitement might cause a relapse," Mom added.

"What does a relapse mean?" Margo asked from the bottom of the stairs.

"It means if Mallory overdoes it, she could get sick again," Dad explained.

"I won't overdo it," I promised. My voice cracked as I spoke and my eyes started to brim with tears. "Please let me go."

"I'm sorry, Mal," Dad said. "But we're staying home."

"What!" the triplets cried. "*We?* We're not going to New York?"

"Now don't you three start," Mom said sternly. "We can't make it this year, and that's that."

"But we'll miss the parade." Nicky's chin was quivering. "And the balloons and floats."

"They'll be there next year," Dad said.

I realized that me and my stupid cooties were ruining Thanksgiving for everyone. I couldn't let that happen.

"Look, Dad," I said, trying to calm my shaky voice, "the parade will be there next year but you may never get bleacher seats again. Why don't you guys go without me?"

Dad held up one hand. "That is out of the question."

"No, really," I continued. "I'll be fine here. You can even get a baby-sitter for me if you want. I'll watch the parade on TV. Maybe I'll see you."

"Now don't be silly." Mom waved her dish towel at me. "Thanksgiving is a time when families are supposed to be together. I could never have a good time knowing you were all alone."

"I wouldn't be alone," I protested. "I'd be with some sitter. Or I could stay with Jessi."

"No." Dad shook his head firmly. "We'll be spending Thanksgiving Day in Stoneybrook, and that's final."

I saw the crestfallen looks on my brothers' and sisters' faces and felt terrible.

"Well, that's great. Just great," I moaned. "Now I've ruined Thanksgiving."

CHAPTER 11

Monday

I can't believe how everything has fallen into place. We raised enough money for the baskets, we did all of our shopping, and we rehearsed the carnival song. It's just amazing. Of course, on Saturday morning, when we were trying to load all those kids into Charlie's car and Mrs. Ramsey's station wagon, I had my doubts about the project...

"Listen up, everybody!" Kristy called to the kids gathered on Jessi's driveway. "We've got a ton of shopping to do, and very little time."

That morning the kids had drawn names out of a hat to see who would go on the shopping trip. Nicky, Vanessa, Charlotte, Becca, Karen, and David Michael were the lucky ones chosen. Claud and the others stayed behind to bake cookies.

Where are we going to shop?" Vanessa asked, as Kristy gave each of them their car assignments. "The mall?"

Kristy shook her head. "The mall has great things but not enough of each item. We're not buying just one apple, we're buying fifty-five. And we're not buying just one book or tape, we're buying lots."

"Boy, it's a good thing I know how to count," Nicky murmured to Becca. "Or else we'd be in big trouble."

Charlotte raised her hand. "Where are we going that we can get that many apples and books?"

Kristy smiled. "Cost-Club. It's a discount shopping mart. And it's *huge*."

"But don't you have to be a member to get in?" Vanessa asked.

"Watson's a member. He lent me his membership card. And Cost-Club agreed to be a sponsor by giving us an extra five percent discount."

Mary Anne consulted her list and said, "Okay, everybody, when we get to Cost-Club, we should divide up. I'll take David Michael and Becca to the food section."

"And I'll take Vanessa and Charlotte to the book section," Jessi said.

"That leaves Nicky and Karen to come with me to look for special presents," Kristy finished up.

"But I want to shop for presents," Becca protested.

"Me too!" David Michael added.

"Me three," said Vanessa.

Kristy thought fast and said, "Okay. After you buy the food and books, we'll all meet in the gift area of the store."

"All right!" David Michael and Nicky gave each other high-fives.

Cost-Club was a gigantic place, bigger than anyone had imagined. It was so vast that some shoppers not only used regular shopping carts, they pulled big wagons down the aisles.

The grocery section took up nearly half of the store. Luckily for Mary Anne, the produce department was close to the main entrance. She let Becca and David Michael push their cart down the rows of fruits and vegetables.

"I've never seen so many apples," Becca

gasped as she stared at a bin piled high with gleaming Macintosh apples. "There must be a million just on that table."

"And two million oranges." David Michael's eyes opened wide as he stood in front of a pyramid of oranges.

But Mary Anne was the one who gasped the loudest. "Look at the prices! At this rate we can get an apple *and* an orange for the baskets. Go ahead, you two, pick them out."

"Don't you want to help us?" Becca asked politely.

"No," Mary Anne said. "This is your project. I want you to choose."

David Michael and Becca took their job very seriously. They deliberated over each apple and orange, muttering things like, "Too mushy. Too small. Nice and shiny. Perfect."

While the kids were counting apples and oranges, Mary Anne discovered a basket of coin-sized chocolates wrapped in gold tinfoil. Each had a picture of a turkey on it. "These are perfect," she cried. Mary Anne counted out three gold medallions for each basket. Then she remembered that some older people are like Stacey and can't eat sweets, so she also filled a paper bag full of sugarless hard candy.

Meanwhile Jessi and her group of kids were standing at the bookshelves.

"This is amazing," Jessi said as she surveyed row upon row of neatly stacked hardcover and paperback books. "There's enough here to start a small library."

"Jessi, look!" Vanessa pointed to a brightly printed sign by a long table piled high with books. "It says, buy four, get one free."

Let's see." Jessi squinted one eye shut. "That means if we need forty books, we'd only have to pay for thirty-two. That's great. Now we need to decide which ones to buy."

"My grandma likes mysteries," Vanessa said, holding up a paperback with a picture of a woman clutching a bloody knife on the cover. "But this looks too gross."

"Why don't we look for mysteries that have nice pictures on the front?" Jessi suggested.

"Yeah," Charlotte agreed. "Pictures of cats are nice. And flowers."

"I like old houses," Vanessa said.

"And I like horses," Jessi added.

It took awhile but they did manage to find a number of mystery books with cats and horses and old houses and flowers on them. Then they relaxed the rules just a little to include candles and pretty women so that they could come up with a total of forty books.

"Now, here's our next assignment," Jessi said. "There are fifteen people at the Manor whose eyesight is so poor that they need to listen to books. Let's check out the recorded books."

"Ooooh! Look!" Charlotte held up a cassette. *The Wind in the Willows*. I love this book."

"That's a kid's book," Vanessa said. "I don't think they'd like it."

"*The Wind in the Willows* is for kids of all ages," Jessi said. "And I think it would be an excellent choice for someone at Stoneybrook Manor."

"Then how about *The Velveteen Rabbit*?" Vanessa said. "I've always loved this story."

"And *Charlotte's Web*." Charlotte hugged the tape to her chest. "I know they'd really, really like this one."

"If we get different tapes, they can trade them and have a lot of stories to listen to," Vanessa suggested.

Jessi nodded. "Even the people who are able to read will have fun listening to these stories."

After their cart was filled with tapes and books, Jessi and the girls looked for Kristy and her group.

"They were going to buy gifts," Jessi said. "I bet they're looking for perfumes and toiletries."

"Nope," Charlotte said. "They're in the toy aisle."

"Toys?" Jessi cocked her head. "That's odd. Well, I guess Kristy must have a reason."

Mary Anne had already found Kristy and the two of them stood surrounded by toy trucks and dolls.

"Hey, Jessi!" Kristy called. "Come over here."

"I bet this really goes fast!" Nicky cried, holding up a small red sports car. He set it on the floor and shoved it toward Vanessa, *"Vrrrooom!"*

Jessi wheeled her cart alongside Mary Anne's and asked, "Did you choose the gifts already?"

Kristy gestured to the children, who were inspecting the toys. "We're doing that now."

"But — "

I know it seems funny buying toys for grandmas and grandpas," Kristy interrupted, "but Nicky pointed out that they could get hand lotion and handkerchiefs any time."

Nicky was testing a paratrooper and his parachute by dropping the toy off of a counter. He called over his shoulder, "How often do people give them fun things? Never."

Kristy grinned at Jessi and shrugged. "I thought about it and it made sense. I mean, I like playing with Play-Doh and Legos, and so does my grandmother — so why wouldn't the residents at Stoneybrook Manor?"

"It'll be like having Christmas a month early!" Karen said, as she contemplated a Barbie doll.

Kristy set a limit on how much each toy could cost, and the children set to work picking out the toys. They tried to guess which one would be right for which person at the home.

"Uncle Joe would probably really like this Popeye bubble blower," Nicky said confidently. "Look, it's got two wands. One for him, and one for me."

"I think Nancy's adopted grandma would like to play jacks and Pick-up Stix." Karen held the two packets in either hand, trying to choose between them. "Of course, she probably likes paper dolls, too."

"Don't you think a Viewmaster would be really neat for someone in a wheelchair?" Charlotte suggested. "They could travel around the world without ever leaving Stoneybrook Manor."

Mary Anne, who can get pretty mushy at moments like this, gave Charlotte a hug. "That would be a lovely gift."

The final purchase was Becca's idea. "We're having a party, aren't we? Why not get party blowers?"

Kristy laughed. "Why not?" she said. "This will be the wildest Thanksgiving party anyone's ever had!"

On Sunday, the kids assembled at Mary Anne's barn to put together the baskets. It was like show-and-tell as the bakers showed their work off to the shoppers.

"Claudia taught us how to make Kooky Cookies," Buddy Barrett said, holding his gingerbread man up for the others to see. The man was green with a horn sticking out of his forehead. "See? I made a Martian."

"I made a Thanksgiving peacock," Melody Korman said. "See how pretty the feathers are?"

Once the shoppers had shared their purchases with the chefs, everyone sat in a circle to put together the baskets. Stacey had asked a local import store to be a sponsor and donate the baskets. It was Claudia's idea for the children to decorate them with ribbons.

Kristy waved a packet of tags in the air. "Mrs. Fellows from Stoneybrook Manor gave me a list of the residents. I want each of you to write a name on your tag, then sign your own name on the other side. Those of you who brought school pictures can put them in the frames Bill and Buddy helped build and place those in the baskets."

Once the artwork was finished, the kids carried their baskets over to the folding tables that the BSC had set up around Mary Anne's barn. One table held oranges. Another apples. Another chocolates. At the table holding the mysteries, Vanessa invented a name game that helped the kids select the books.

"The perfect book for Mrs. Brookes," Vanessa chanted, "is the one that's titled *Too Many Crooks*."

"Here's a book for Herman Schwartz," Bill Korman said, as he held up a book with a frog on the cover. "A picture of a frog with warts."

"*Candle, Candle, Burning Bright* is just the book for Mary Wright," chanted Charlotte, joining in the rhyming party.

The toys were the hit of the day as each child picked just the right present for his or her basket. Once they were done, the children stacked all fifty-five baskets on one table and Jessi took a picture of them with her instant camera. "We'll show this to Mal. I know it'll cheer her up."

With the shopping done and the baskets assembled, there was only one more project to finish — the carnival. Stacey supervised that, and showed Kristy and the others the results Monday after school.

"We decided to limit the carnival to a Bean Bag Throw, a Cakewalk, and Go Fish," Stacey explained. "And we'll start things off with a singalong led by Carolyn and Marilyn." She smiled at the Arnold twins. "Why don't you two teach your song to us?"

Marilyn spoke first. "We were going to see if there were words to 'Turkey in the Straw,' but we couldn't find any. Then we tried to find a Pilgrim song at the library but all of the Thanksgiving books were checked out."

"So," Carolyn cut in, "we decided to find a song that showed how we felt about our project. And that's when Marilyn suggested we sing 'The Friend Song.' "

"You probably already know it," Marilyn said, dividing the groups into three. "It's a round. We'll sing it several times and you join in when you're sure of the words."

Kristy would never have admitted it, but listening to the kids' voices was really moving. When the round ended, she put her arms around Marilyn and Carolyn and announced, "This is going to be the best Thanksgiving party ever."

CHAPTER 12

You know the expression, "A watched pot never boils"? Well, a watched clock never ticks. It was late Tuesday afternoon and I had been staring at the alarm clock next to my bed for what seemed like forever. I was waiting for five-thirty. That's when the kids would be returning from Stoneybrook Manor. I couldn't wait to hear how the party had gone.

"Mom?" I called from the door of my bedroom. "Any sign of Margo and the others?"

"No, honey," she replied from the living room downstairs. "But the program isn't over until five. Then the mothers have to drive the kids home. So it'll be awhile."

I decided not to watch my clock anymore and tried to read one of the books Jessi had checked out of the library. It was a funny book called *Lucy Berky and the Thanksgiving Turkey* and it was about a farm girl who befriends a wild turkey. Together they plot to free all of the turkeys in Hooterville the day before Thanksgiving.

Even though the book was silly, I read it all the way to the end and even felt like cheering when the people of Hooterville vowed to eat cheese pizza instead of turkey on Thanksgiving Day. When I finally set the book down on my bedside table I couldn't believe how the time had flown. It was almost six o'clock and, as if on cue, I heard the front door open and the sound of voices in the foyer.

"Mallory, we're home!" Nicky shouted from downstairs.

"Boy, did we have fun!" Margo cried.

I listened to the rumble of feet galloping up the stairs. Suddenly my room was filled with my brothers and sisters. They wore grins that stretched from ear to ear.

Vanessa rushed to sit on my bed. "Oh, Mallory, the party was just wonderful."

"We saw Uncle Joe," Nicky said. "And you should have seen him blowing bubbles. They were everywhere."

Adam clutched his stomach and said, "One popped on Mrs. Carver's head, but she didn't mind. She just laughed and laughed. So did everybody."

"Karen Brewer and Esther Bernard started playing jacks right in the middle of the room,"

Margo said. "Pretty soon everyone wanted to take a turn."

I held up my hands. "Wait a minute. Wait. I want to know every little thing that happened. So would you guys start at the beginning?"

"You mean, when we first went to Mary Anne's to plan this party?" Nicky asked. "Or when we met at the barn after school today and got in the vans?"

"Start with the vans."

Byron took a deep breath. "Mrs. Brewer, Mrs. Kishi, and Charlie Thomas drove us to Stoneybrook Manor."

"Charlotte and Becca rode with me," Margo said.

Vanessa waved a hand in the air. "Let's skip over how we got there and who rode in what car, and go right to the good part."

"What was the good part?" I asked.

Claire folded her arms across her chest and said, "Walking in the front door."

"They were waiting for us in the lobby," Vanessa explained. "With big smiles on their faces. There were two white-haired ladies and a couple of bald men in wheelchairs and a lot of people with walkers that have these cloth bags hanging off the handles."

"What's in the bags?" I asked.

Vanessa shrugged. "I'm not sure."

"A comb, two packs of Certs, a roll of quarters, and a photo of the grandchildren," Nicky replied. "That's what Mrs. Lymon carries in her bag. I know 'cause I asked her."

"What happened after you said hello? Did you hand out your goody baskets?"

"There was a little bit of confusion at first," Jordan said. "We didn't know where to go."

"Then Mrs. Fellows — she's the nice lady in charge of activities — met us and took us to the multi-purpose room," Vanessa said.

"That took a long time," Claire added, "because old people are slow. Even in their wheelchairs, they're slow. And it was kind of hot in there."

I nodded, remembering how warm the building always was when we visited Uncle Joe. "I think they keep the thermostat turned up because old people get cold pretty easily."

"Yeah," Nicky said. "Most of them had sweaters on and blankets over their knees."

"Once everyone was in a circle," Vanessa continued, "Kristy told us to skip around them."

"Then we stopped behind the chairs of the people whose names we'd drawn," Byron cut in. "Luckily, Mrs. Fellows asked them to wear name tags, so we didn't get confused."

"After that we handed out the baskets and

yelled Happy Thanksgiving!" Nicky said.

"And everyone thanked us," Vanessa added.

"One woman told me that the basket was the nicest present she'd ever gotten in her entire life," Margo said.

Claire nodded. "Practically everyone said that. Mrs. Wright laughed when she saw the Miss Piggy puzzle I'd picked for her. Then we put it together. Twice."

"Mr. Hamilton looked at his box of Legos and just kept saying, 'I'm touched. I am so touched,' " Adam said. "He built a bridge and a castle."

"I wish I could have been there," I murmured. "Just to see their faces when they got the toys and books."

"Then Mrs. Fellows took us to visit the people who had to stay in bed," Claire said. "I felt bad for them. They seemed so sick."

I squeezed Claire's hand. "I'm sure it meant a lot to have you visit."

Claire smiled. "One woman didn't say anything about the basket, she just held my hand and her eyes got all watery."

"A little old man named Mr. Renquist let me turn the crank on his bed," Nicky added. "First I raised his head, then his feet. Then both. He said he felt like he was caught inside an accordion. It was pretty funny."

Hearing them tell their stories of the people in their hospital beds made me realize how lucky I was. I had been in bed for nearly a month but those people would probably spend the rest of their lives that way.

"When we got back to the multi-purpose room," Vanessa continued, "Kristy announced that it was now time for the Thanksgiving Carnival to begin."

"What did they think of that?"

"Well, a few didn't hear her right," Jordan replied. "One man, who had a hearing aid attached to a battery, said really loudly, 'No, thanks, I can't eat caramels.'"

"It took a little while for them to understand what was happening," Byron said. "But as soon as they understood, everyone wanted to go first."

Nicky grinned. "We let Uncle Joe be the first to toss the bean bag and he got it in the turkey's mouth three times in a row! The other old guys all cheered."

Claire leaned on my bed with her elbows by my pillow. "The Cakewalk was funny because hardly anybody walked. They were all in those chairs but I think they were happy."

"I worked on the Go Fish booth," Margo said. "The people would dangle their lines over the edge of the screen and we'd attach cookies that Claudia had baked and some of the little chocolate coins from Cost-Club to their hooks. And people loved them."

Jordan grinned. "Bart Bartlesby, the oldest man at the home, kept shouting, 'Oh, I think you landed a big one!' and everyone would laugh."

"What did Mrs. Fellows think of the party?" I asked.

"I didn't hear her say anything," Vanessa said. "But she did a lot of hugging."

"No kidding." Nicky wrinkled his nose. "She hugged everybody *twice*. After the first time, David Michael and us guys ran from her and hid behind the Go Fish screen."

"Did she see you?" I asked.

Nicky shrugged. "I guess so. But she just laughed. Everybody was laughing a lot. Especially when we sang our song."

"You sang a song?" I asked as I fluffed up my pillow. "When?"

"At the very end," Vanessa said. "Kristy asked us to form a circle. Then she made a speech about Thanksgiving, and what this day meant to all of us. And then we sang our friendship song that Marilyn and Carolyn taught us."

I clasped my hands behind my head. "It sounds like it was a perfect party."

Nicky hopped off the bed. "Yeah. Most of us promised to come back for more visits. Mr.

Renquist said next time I can crank up the middle of his bed. He says that looks *really* funny."

"Claire and I promised to visit all of our new friends at least once a month. And we will, too." Margo turned to Claire. "Right?"

Claire bobbed her head in one firm nod. "Right."

I leaned back against my pillows with a sigh. "I hope someday I can go with you."

"Then you can play jacks with Mrs. Bernard," Claire said.

"Or Legos with Mr. Hamilton," Adam added.

"That sounds wonderful." I stifled a yawn. I couldn't believe I was getting tired again. The excitement of hearing about their visit had worn me out.

Vanessa caught my yawn and hustled the others out of the room. "Come on, you guys," she said. "Mal needs to take a nap. And I need to do my homework. I have a test tomorrow and then — " Vanessa paused and grinned at the others.

"No more school!" Everybody shouted.

"That's right." I smiled to myself. "One more day until Thanksgiving." Even though the trip to New York had been canceled, I was looking forward to spending the holiday with my family.

CHAPTER 13

"Who wants to polish the silver?" Mom called from the kitchen.

"We'll do it," Adam said, volunteering himself and Byron and Jordan. "Can we polish the big carving knives too?"

"Yes, but be careful," Mother said as she carried the heavy mahogany box into the dining room.

Wednesday had been a half day at school and everyone was spending the afternoon preparing for Thanksgiving dinner.

Where was I? Flat on my back on the couch, of course. But I was dressed and I'd even put on the earrings Jessi had given me when we first got our ears pierced. I was doing everything I could to try to feel part of the festivities.

"Mom, can I fold napkins or something?" I called as my mother scurried through the living room. She was carrying the white linen tablecloth that had belonged to her mother and

115

her mother's mother before that.

"Sorry, Mal, but Margo and Nicky have that covered."

"What about ironing the tablecloth?"

"That's my job," she said. "Your job is to relax on the couch."

"I hate lying on the couch," I complained. "I feel like a slug."

Mom smiled sympathetically. "Maybe we can find a job for you. One that isn't too tiring."

"Thanks." I tried to sound grateful but I didn't feel quite that way. I had hoped that this holiday would be fun. And it was. For everyone but me. I was just an observer. I wanted to participate.

I watched Margo parade through the living room with the ceramic turkey centerpiece that we used year after year. Claire followed behind with a box of little plaster Indians and Pilgrims in her arms.

Last Thanksgiving we'd spent hours setting up a colonial village in the center of the dining room table. Byron and Jordan had broken off sprigs of evergreen to make trees, and Nicky and Adam had collected pebbles for the village walls. I remembered that they'd found a huge round rock that we placed outside the village. Using orange and black watercolors, I'd painted the words, Plymouth Rock, on it. Now that rock was part of the permanent collection.

I listened numbly as my brothers and sisters argued over the placement of each rock and twig, and what food the Pilgrims would eat. Nobody cared whether I helped with the village. No one even asked for my opinion. It was as if I were invisible.

Before I could get completely depressed, Mom reappeared. She was carrying scissors, some stiff paper, and a package of Magic Markers. "I've found just the job for you," she said cheerily. "Place cards."

"Place cards?" I repeated, sitting up. "Do you just want me to write our names on them?"

Mom moved a tray table next to the couch. "You can decorate them any way you want. Use your imagination and have fun."

This did sound like fun. And I was glad to think about something other than myself. I set to work cutting out the little cards and decorating them. I thought about each member of my family and tried to make the place card reflect his or her personality. Since Vanessa likes poetry, I made hers flowery. I drew teddy bears and dolls on Claire's. I tried to draw Frodo, our hamster, on Nicky's, but it ended up looking like a bear, too. So I added a few frogs and snakes. For the triplets, I drew the Three Musketeers' hats with a different-colored plume in each hat. While I was mulling over what to draw on the rest of the cards, the doorbell rang.

"I'll get that!" shrieked Margo. She bolted out of her chair and raced to the front door so fast that I got the funny feeling she'd been expecting the bell to ring.

The next thing I knew, I heard shuffling feet and lots of whispering and giggling in the hallway. Then Kristy appeared in the living room, surrounded by the rest of the BSC members and about ten kids.

"Surprise!" they cried.

I nearly knocked over my tray table from the shock. "What's going on?" I asked.

Claire, who had disappeared when the doorbell rang, squeezed through the group. She placed a basket next to the couch. It was filled with fruits and chocolates, books and a photograph.

"This basket was made for you by all of us. It is a small — " Claire paused and looked at the ceiling, trying to remember her speech. She moved her lips silently, re-reciting what she had just said and then she continued. "It is a small token of our steam."

Vanessa whispered in her ear and Claire blushed. "Oops, I meant, our *es*-teem."

"Thanks!" I exclaimed.

"Wait!" Buddy Barrett called. "There's more."

The kids parted and in marched Stacey, carrying a cardboard turkey. She was followed by Becca, Karen, and David Michael, who held a screen painted to look like an ocean and a fishing pole.

Stacey handed me the pole. "Since you couldn't make it to the party, we thought we'd bring the party to you. So Go Fish."

"What?" I giggled.

Nicky stepped forward to advise me. "Throw your string over the screen and Bill Korman will tie a present to it."

Claire whispered, "It's probably going to be a cookie."

I did as I was told and cast my fishing line over the screen. Claudia hurriedly joined Bill and after a great deal of whispering and tugging on the string, Bill shouted, "Pull 'er up. I think you landed a big one!"

I did get a Kooky Cookie, but a surprise was attached to it.

"Look," Becca Ramsey cried. "Mal's gingerbread lady is wearing earrings. Real ones."

Claudia peeked over the screen. "These are very special, magical earrings. The person who puts them on will be instantly cured."

"I wish," I murmured, as I examined her

creations. They were little wooden bottles with hand-painted labels that read, *Miracul Cure*. (I knew then Claud really had made them herself. But that made them even more special.)

I removed my earrings and put on Claud's. "I feel better already!" I exclaimed. "It is a miracle."

The Bean Bag Toss was next. Buddy and Karen held the turkey while I threw the bean bag. The first bean bag hit the turkey in the eye, the second in the chest. Finally I got one in his mouth.

Mary Anne gave me my prize. "One bean bag gets a bag of jelly beans," she said, handing me a large bag of gourmet jelly beans. I passed the bag around the room and even sampled a few myself. Tangerine, coconut, and double chocolate. "Heaven!" I declared.

While the rest of us devoured the jelly beans, Kristy was busily placing numbers made of construction paper on our living room floor. She made a crazy course from the doorway to the armchair, around a table, and back to the door. "The Cakewalk is tricky. It's usually played by people who can walk — "

"Or roll," Margo cut in. "Like Mr. Hamilton in his wheelchair."

"That's right, Margo." Kristy laughed. "In

your case, Mal, we decided that you could pick a stand-in."

"Like in baseball?" Buddy asked.

"Exactly. But instead of a pinch hitter or runner, Mal is going to pick a pinch walker. Okay, Mal, who's it going to be?"

"I think I'll pick Jessi," I said, "since she's my best friend and has stood by me through sick and thin."

Jessi groaned at my joke but lined up with the kids, who each stood on a number. Then Kristy pushed the button on the tape recorder she'd brought and we listened to Raffi sing "Walk Around the Block" as the kids danced from number to number.

When Kristy pressed stop, Claudia, who was holding a special cake in the shape of a turkey, checked the bottom of the cake for the number Mary Anne had taped there earlier.

"And the winner of the Pike Cakewalk," Claudia announced, "is Number 14. Number 14."

Everyone lifted first one foot and then the other to check what number they were standing on. Then Vanessa yelled, "I won. I won! I've never won anything."

Claudia handed her the cake and then Vanessa turned right around and handed it to me. "Happy Thanksgiving, sis."

121

I was so touched that I couldn't speak. But before the tears could blur my eyes, Jessi said, "As our final presentation we'd like to sing the song we sang at Stoneybrook Manor. I think it has an extra special meaning now that we're singing it to you, Mallory."

Marilyn and Carolyn Arnold quickly arranged the kids in three groups. "Ready, everybody?" Carolyn asked. The kids nodded and the round began.

"Make new friends
but keep the old;
One is silver
And the other's gold."

I hadn't had a chance to cry after the Cakewalk, but now I cried. Big, happy tears.

CHAPTER 14

Thanksgiving Day. At last! I awoke to the most wonderful aroma on earth — baking bread. The smell was so delicious that I hopped out of bed, slipped into my robe and scurried down the stairs.

Mom was in the kitchen filling a big pot with water. We were going to have mashed potatoes. *Mmmm!* I like to eat mashed potatoes any time of the year, but for some reason they always taste extra good on Thanksgiving. It probably has a lot to do with the turkey and gravy that's served with them.

Two pumpkin pies stood cooling on a rack by the window. The crystal water glasses were lined up on the counter, and Mom's best china plates were stacked neatly on the sideboard.

"Everything looks and smells terrific," I murmured.

"Mallory! You're up," Mom said as she set the pot on the stove and dropped the peeled potatoes into the water. "Happy Thanksgiving."

I shuffled across the kitchen floor and gave her a hug. "Happy Thanksgiving to you! You look really pretty."

Mom smiled. Then she self-consciously patted the back of her hair. Mom had gone to the beauty shop (something she does only for special occasions) and her hair did look nice. Also, she was wearing her red knit dress. She'd tied her best red and green plaid taffeta apron over it. The apron had ruffles all around it and was so fancy, it was hard to imagine it functioning as a real apron with mashed potato glops and gravy smears on it.

"Mallory, come look," Vanessa called to me from the living room. She was kneeling by the coffee table with a large piece of poster board. "I've drawn up our official Thanksgiving menu."

Vanessa had been practicing her calligraphy, so the menu looked very fancy. And Mom had helped her with the spelling. It was perfect. Here's what she'd written:

Thanksgiving Dinner
chez la Pikes

Appetizers
Vegetable Dip   Cheese Log
Stuffed Mushrooms

Salad
Green Leaf with Cherry Tomatoes

Main Course
Roast Turkey
Wild Rice-and-Chestnut Stuffing
Mashed Potatoes and Gravy
Buttered Green Peas
Pearled Onions in Cream Sauce
Cranberry Sauce

Dessert
Pumpkin Pie and Vanilla Ice Cream

Just reading it made me ravenously hungry. Which was a good sign. For the last couple of weeks I'd hardly had any appetite.

"Vanessa, that looks like a menu from a fancy restaurant," I said.

"Do you really think so?"

"Absolutely."

Music suddenly filled the house. Dad entered the living room, waving one finger like a conductor. "Ah, Pachelbel's 'Canon,' " he said, and sighed. "Just beautiful."

It's a tradition at our house to listen only to classical music on Thanksgiving. And no television is allowed except for one program —

the Macy's parade. (However, my brothers have started to fudge on the rule and watch football.)

Ring!

"Let me get it!" Claire bounced through the living room in her best dress, which was green velveteen with a white collar and cuffs.

"Happy Turkey Day," Claire called into the phone in the hallway. For the next three minutes she held the receiver to her ear and either said, "Uh-huh," or just nodded.

"Claire," Dad whispered. "Who is it?"

She held out the receiver to Dad. "I'm not sure."

"Happy Thanksgiving," Dad said into the phone. Then, "Phil? Good to hear from you. Hold on." He covered the receiver with his hand and called to Mom in the kitchen. "Hey, it's the Strausses. They're calling from a pay phone. The parade's about to start and they wanted to let us know they're thinking of us."

Mom hurried into the hall. "Isn't that sweet!"

"Who's on the phone?" Byron asked from the top of the stairs. He was dressed in maroon corduroy slacks, a yellow shirt, and a blue-and-yellow sweater that he'd gotten for Christmas the year before. "Is it Grandma?"

"No," Mom answered. "We're calling her

126

after dinner this afternoon. It's Phil and Marie in New York City."

"Tell them we're going to watch for them on TV," Adam said, joining Byron at the top of the stairs. He too, was wearing his best holiday clothes.

I stared down at my pajamas and made a beeline for the stairs. I wasn't about to spend Thanksgiving Day in my robe. I had a new outfit for special occasions, such as a party or a dance. It's a blue velvet skirt with a matching bolero jacket and a white silk blouse. I was a little afraid to wear it when I'd be eating, but I decided not to worry about it, and to take a chance.

I pulled my hair into a pony tail and tied a white satin ribbon around it. When I looked in the mirror, I decided that I looked pretty good, considering the circumstances.

"The parade starts in five minutes," Nicky announced, marching up and down the hall past the bedrooms. "Five minutes till the parade."

We assembled in the family room and watched the Macy's parade from start to finish, munching on *hors d'oeuvres* of crackers and cheese, stuffed mushrooms, and vegetables dipped in ranch dressing.

Dad made a game of voting for our favorite

float, favorite giant balloon, and favorite celebrity. Everyone voted for a dinosaur float that actually *walked*. I have no idea how they made it do that!

Nicky has always loved the Popeye balloon, but everyone voted differently for that category. My personal favorite was Clifford the Big Red Dog.

Santa Claus was the clear winner in the celebrity category.

We had a lot of fun and it was almost as nice as being at the parade in person. Almost. The one consolation was pointed out by Jordan later that afternoon.

"Hey, I just remembered. The cameras didn't show the Strausses or any of the people sitting in the bleachers by Macy's. If we'd gone to New York we wouldn't have been on television."

"That's right," Nicky said. "Now I don't feel so bad."

When the parade was over it was time to set the table. I wanted to help but my parents wouldn't let me. They thought I'd already had too much activity just walking around the house. I lay on the couch while my brothers and sisters circled the table, setting the dinner and salad plates in front of the place cards. I closed my eyes and listened to the clink of silverware and the sound of plates sliding onto our linen tablecloth. It was a nice comforting sound.

At two o'clock, Mom rang a crystal bell. That was the signal for us to take our seats. There was one uncomfortable moment when Mom and Dad seriously considered making me eat on the couch in the living room.

"You *have* to let me sit at the table," I pleaded. "I feel bad enough that we missed our trip to New York. Please don't make me miss the meal, too."

After a hurried discussion, they finally decided that I could sit at the dining room table, but only if I reclined on a lawn chair.

"I know it seems silly," Mom told me, "but the excitement of this day could really tire you out. It usually exhausts me and I'm not even sick."

Once we were in our places, Margo insisted we sing a song she learned about Thanksgiving called, "Come, Ye Thankful People, Come." Dad reminded us that that song had been around for hundreds of years and could have been sung by the Pilgrims themselves. It gave me goose bumps to think that, even before we were the United States of America, people just like us would gather around a table and celebrate the harvest by sharing food with their family.

This Thanksgiving my parents had bought

several bottles of sparkling cider (which looks just like champagne and has bubbles that tickle your nose) and Mom carefully filled the crystal goblets by each of our plates. Then Dad stood up and said, "I'd like to propose a toast." He cleared his throat and said, "May the roof above us never fall in, and may all of us below never fall out."

Then we clinked glasses, which could be pretty dangerous in our rowdy family, but nothing broke. In fact, my brothers and sisters and I felt really grown-up.

After the toast, Dad carved the turkey and we each put in our requests.

"I'd like white meat, please," I said.

"I want half-dark and half-white," Nicky said. "And a drumstick."

Dad chuckled. "Why don't you start with the drumstick, and then we'll see about seconds."

Mom removed the lids from the bowls holding the potatoes and peas and onions, and steam filled the air. After a flurry of plate passing, and of requesting butter and the gravy boat, and more bread, the room suddenly fell almost silent. The only sound was the munching of ten very contented people.

I finished my plate and even had seconds of (surprise) mashed potatoes and gravy.

Nicky actually finished his drumstick and managed to eat a small helping of dark meat. We made it through the meal without one person breaking a glass, or spilling milk, or even dropping a fork. It was amazing!

"Who's ready for pumpkin pie?" Mom said, after she checked her watch. "It looks like it's just about time."

I was surprised to hear that we were on a schedule until I heard the doorbell ringing. Dad looked at Mom and grinned mischievously. "Now I wonder who that might be?"

From the tone in his voice I could tell that Dad knew full well who it was, but Mom played along with him.

"Gee, I don't know *who* would come visit at this hour," she replied. "Nicky, why don't you let our visitors in while Vanessa and I dish out the pie."

Visitors?" I repeated. "Now?"

Claudia was the first to enter the dining room. "We heard you guys had some extra pumpkin pie at your house."

"Do you mind if we join you?" asked Mary Anne, who was behind Claud.

"Yeah." Kristy stuck her head in the doorway. "I'm starved."

Jessi's face appeared over Kristy's shoulder. "Me, too."

Stacey waved from the back. "No pie for me, thanks. But I did hear you had some outstanding stuffed mushrooms."

"You guys!" I shook my head in amazement. "I can't believe you left your families to be with me."

Kristy shrugged. "The fact of the matter is, we're expecting a phone call and we want to be sure not to miss it."

She pointed to our phone and, I'm not kidding, it rang. It was like magic. Even Kristy looked surprised, but she didn't miss a beat. She just said, "There she is now."

You'll never guess who was on the phone. Dawn. Calling all the way from California.

I held the receiver so Kristy and the others could put their heads close to it and listen in.

"Happy Thanksgiving!" Dawn shouted. "I wish I were with you. It's seventy degrees here. It doesn't even feel like Thanksgiving. More like the Fourth of July."

We took turns telling Dawn how much we missed her, and everyone promised to write. Then the call was over and it was time for pumpkin pie.

Dessert was served in the living room because our dining room is barely big enough for ten people. Fifteen is impossible. I lay on the couch eating my pie, surrounded by my family and closest friends. We chattered non-stop for two hours.

I know I didn't get to go to New York and stay in a fancy hotel. And I didn't get to watch the parade from those special bleachers. But that night it didn't matter. I went to sleep feeling happier than I'd felt in weeks.

CHAPTER 15

Ring!

On Friday morning the phone woke me up. It was Mom's cousin Marie.

"Mallory, how are you feeling?" she asked when I answered.

"Much better," I replied. "But I wish we could have watched the parade with you."

"Me too," Marie said. "But if it makes you feel any better, the weather was kind of lousy. Halfway through it started to drizzle. I was afraid we were going to have a real downpour."

"Still, it would have been nice to be in New York and see all the decorations."

"That's what I'm calling about," Marie said. "Put your mom on the line, will you?"

Then Marie invited Mom and my family to come to New York on Saturday for lunch and shopping. It sounded like a lot of fun. Of course, I couldn't go, but Margo, Vanessa,

Claire, and Nicky went with Mom. The triplets decided they wanted to stay home to watch football and play with their friends.

It was cozy being home with just Dad and the triplets. On Saturday afternoon, Dad made a bowl of popcorn and we watched as the first snow began to fall. Winter had arrived and Christmas was just around the corner.

The next morning everything was covered in a sparkling blanket of white. The sun shone brightly and I felt great. Well, maybe not great, but better than I'd felt in a month. I got dressed, ate breakfast at the table, and actually caught up with some of my homework.

Sunday afternoon the doorbell rang and I was surprised to discover Jessi and Kristy standing on our front doorstep. Kristy held a manila envelope in her hand.

"We've been working on our new advertising campaign," she said as she took off her coat. "But we wanted to talk to you first, before we did anything."

"Kristy thought, with Christmas only a month away, it would be a great time to post new advertisements," Jessi explained as Kristy opened the envelope and pulled out a sheet of white paper.

"Claud designed the new flier." Kristy held up the drawing. It was a holiday design with holly and ivy around the border.

"It's wonderful," I said. "Her best yet."

"It's finished except for one thing," Kristy said, pointing to the paper. "Your name."

"Claud is going to list every BSC member's name at the bottom," Jessi said. "And she'd be happy to list you as an honorary member — "

"But we think we know how you feel about that," Kristy added. "So we won't list your name if you don't want us to."

This was it. The moment of truth had arrived. I didn't know how long it would be before my parents would let me rejoin the club. What if they said I never could?

I took a deep breath. "The mono could stretch on for another month or two, according to Dr. Dellenkamp. And even if I do get better soon, Mom and Dad may not let me come back to the BSC. At least not right away. That's an awfully long time to be absent."

Jessi and Kristy nodded but kept silent. It was absolute agony for me to say it but I did. "You'd better not put my name on the new flier. Or on any future advertisements or letters."

Jessi sighed and took my hand. "I know that was a tough decision to make, Mal."

Kristy nodded. "But we'll honor your wish."

I bit my lip and added, "You should probably start looking for a replacement for me."

Kristy patted my shoulder. "I don't think we're going to start a big search, but if someone great wants to join the club — if he or she comes to *us* — then we might consider it."

I knew leaving the club was the right thing to do, but it hurt. A deep, aching kind of hurt. I was getting better. But clearly it was going to take time before I was completely well. Maybe a lot of time. I didn't even know when I'd be able to go back to school. All I could do was wait.

About the Author

ANN M. MARTIN did *a lot* of baby-sitting when she was growing up in Princeton, New Jersey. She is a former editor of books for children, and was graduated from Smith College.

Ms. Martin lives in New York City with her cats, Mouse and Rosie. She likes ice cream and *I Love Lucy*; and she hates to cook.

Ann Martin's Apple Paperbacks include *Yours Turly, Shirley; Ten Kids, No Pets; With You and Without You; Bummer Summer;* and all the other books in the Baby-sitters Club series.

Look for #70

STACEY AND THE CHEERLEADERS

"Hey, I'm starving. Let's get something to eat," RJ suggested, his face suddenly brightening. "How about Pizza Express?"

I have about three or four favorite places to eat in Stoneybrook. The Pizza Express is not one of them. But I was dying to get out of that theater. "Sure," I said.

In the lobby, RJ called his dad to let him know where we were going. I stretched my legs and let myself air out.

Sabrina saw me again and waved. She had that envious look in her eyes. Somehow, that didn't affect me the way it had earlier. I was busy evaluating my date. I gave it a 3 on a scale of 1 (worst) to 10 (best). RJ was okay in some ways, but I could tell we weren't made for each other.

I was feeling depressed as we walked out of the theater. I guess I had built the date up too much in advance.

Well, guess who was in the Pizza Express that night? The Group. Just about the entire cheerleading squad and the basketball team, taking up four tables and having a great time.

"Hey, Blazemeister!" Marty Bukowski called out to RJ.

"The Bukeman!" RJ returned.

RJ took my arm and we walked to Marty's table. Everyone turned to us and shouted hi. I have never seen so many toothpaste-ad smiles in my life. Sheila was pulling over a couple of chairs from a nearby empty table.

Boy, was my mood changing. A few days ago, none of these kids would have given me a second look. Now they were moving aside to let me sit down.

**Don't miss any of the latest books
in the Baby-sitters Club series
by Ann M. Martin**

THE BABY-SITTERS CLUB®

by Ann M. Martin

More titles... ▶

☐ MG44970-2	#49 Claudia and the Genius of Elm Street	$3.25
☐ MG44969-9	#50 Dawn's Big Date	$3.25
☐ MG44968-0	#51 Stacey's Ex-Best Friend	$3.25
☐ MG44966-4	#52 Mary Anne + 2 Many Babies	$3.25
☐ MG44967-2	#53 Kristy for President	$3.25
☐ MG44965-6	#54 Mallory and the Dream Horse	$3.25
☐ MG44964-8	#55 Jessi's Gold Medal	$3.25
☐ MG45657-1	#56 Keep Out, Claudia!	$3.25
☐ MG45658-X	#57 Dawn Saves the Planet	$3.25
☐ MG45659-8	#58 Stacey's Choice	$3.25
☐ MG45660-1	#59 Mallory Hates Boys (and Gym)	$3.25
☐ MG45662-8	#60 Mary Anne's Makeover	$3.50
☐ MG45663-6	#61 Jessi's and the Awful Secret	$3.50
☐ MG45664-4	#62 Kristy and the Worst Kid Ever	$3.50
☐ MG45665-2	#63 Claudia's ~~Freind~~ Friend	$3.50
☐ MG45666-0	#64 Dawn's Family Feud	$3.50
☐ MG45667-9	#65 Stacey's Big Crush	$3.50
☐ MG45575-3	Logan's Story Special Edition Readers' Request	$3.25
☐ MG44240-6	Baby-sitters on Board! Super Special #1	$3.95
☐ MG44239-2	Baby-sitters' Summer Vacation Super Special #2	$3.95
☐ MG43973-1	Baby-sitters' Winter Vacation Super Special #3	$3.95
☐ MG42493-9	Baby-sitters' Island Adventure Super Special #4	$3.95
☐ MG43575-2	California Girls! Super Special #5	$3.95
☐ MG43576-0	New York, New York! Super Special #6	$3.95
☐ MG44963-X	Snowbound Super Special #7	$3.95
☐ MG44962-X	Baby-sitters at Shadow Lake Super Special #8	$3.95
☐ MG45661-X	Starring the Baby-sitters Club Super Special #9	$3.95

Available wherever you buy books...or use this order form.

Scholastic Inc., P.O. Box 7502, 2931 E. McCarty Street, Jefferson City, MO 65102

Please send me the books I have checked above. I am enclosing $_____
(please add $2.00 to cover shipping and handling). Send check or money order - no
cash or C.O.D.s please.

Name _____

Address _____

City_____ State/Zip _____

Please allow four to six weeks for delivery. Offer good in the U.S. only. Sorry, mail orders are not
available to residents of Canada. Prices subject to change.

Don't miss out on
The All New

How would *YOU* like to visit Universal Studios in Orlando, Florida?

Check out the sights!

Experience the rides!

Tour the Studios!

Enter  **THE BABY-SITTERS CLUB** ®

Summer Super Special Giveaway for your chance to win!

We'll send one grand prize winner and a parent or guardian on an all expense paid trip to Universal Studios in Orlando, Florida for 3 days and 2 nights!

25 second prize winners receive a Baby-sitters Club Fun Pack filled with a Baby-sitters Club T-Shirt, "Songs For My Best Friends" cassette, Baby-sitters Club stationery and more!

All you have to do is fill out the coupon below or write the information on a 3" x 5" piece of paper and mail to:

THE BABY-SITTERS CLUB SUMMER SUPER SPECIAL GIVEAWAY P.O. Box 7500, Jefferson City, MO 65102. Return by November 30 1993.

THE SUMMER SUPER SPECIAL GIVEAWAY

Name_____ Birthdate _____

Address _____

City_____ State/Zip _____

Create Your Own Mystery Stories!

MYSTERY GAME!

WHO: Boyfriend   **WHY:** Romance

WHAT: Phone Call   **WHERE:** Dance

Use the special Mystery Case card to pick WHO did it, WHAT was involved, WHY it happened and WHERE it happened. Then dial secret words on your Mystery Wheels to add to the story! Travel around the special Stoneybrook map gameboard to uncover your friends' secret word clues! Finish four baby-sitting jobs and find out all the words to win. Then have everyone join in to tell the story!